Wall of Flowers

....

Shelia Smith

Contents

Chapter 1

A very cursed inwardly as she trudged through the rain. She narrowly avoided being splashed by an oncoming car as she pulled on her hoodie strings, and consequently felt her hair stick to her face.

She had carpooled with Carson this morning instead of going on her own as she usually did and now that he had football practice, she was left to walk home alone. Luckily, her home wasn't too far away, but it was raining cats and dogs and her distaste for dirty water prevented her from just running to her house. She contemplated it for quite some time but then decided that getting out of the rain quickly was not worth the yucky and itching feeling she would endure in the process.

The air was cold and the wind against her wet clothes made her shiver. Her home wasn't much far left to go.

If she squinted, she was able to decipher the outline of her average-sized house.

"I swear if I end up getting a cold," she sighed to herself, "I'll rip Carson to shreds."

Avery's immune system wasn't the greatest and she knew this. She probably spent about 50-60% of her eighteen years being sick. If you were wondering why she didn't at least have an umbrella: she did, but when she had looked for it she only realised it was in her car.

The car she didn't take.

Because Carson offered to take her.

Okay, maybe Avery wasn't the best at planning things out and being organised. She could be a bit scatter-brained at times and easily flustered as a result. But she was just human like the rest of us.

A couple of minutes had passed and Avery had finally reached her driveway, much to her relief. A grateful sigh escaped her lips but it was then that the rain had decided to ease to a slight drizzle. She rolled her eyes as she removed the hood and fixed her fuzzed-up hair. The weather just couldn't have better timing, could it?

Avery liked rainy weather, but not when she was caught in it. She preferred it when she could curl up in her reading nook and stare out the window, accompanied by a cup of tea and a great novel. It made her feel as if she was the main character in an indie film.

She used her keys to unlock the door, opened it and walked inside. Greeted by the scent of freshly baked cookies, she took a deep breath and allowed the smell to calm her annoyance at the previous weather.

"Maman, papa! Je suis ici !" she announced her presence at the doorway, removing her sneakers and placing them on the mat. "I smell cookies!" {Mom, dad! I'm here!}

"Bonjour, Doux-Doux. The cookies are for after dinner," her mother stuck her head out from the kitchen, her expression donning her usual cheery smile. "Oh my goodness! Avery Toussaint, you are drenched!"

Her mother rushed over to her, a concerned look etched on her face. Her apron was spotted with flour as she attempted to help Avery remove her hoodie. "You know you'll get sick! Go run upstairs and take a warm bath. I'll tell your papa to pick up some medicine on his way home."

"Alright, alright," Avery muttered as she was being shooed by her doting maman.

Mrs Toussaint watched her daughter hurry up the stairs, curls bouncing wildly. She put a hand to her head and sighed.

"What am I going to do with her?" she asked herself.
****

Around the table, the small family ate their dinner in comfortable silence. Avery sniffled, quickly drawing her parents' attention to her.

"Tu as oublié ton parapluie?" her father tilted his head to the side. {You forgot your umbrella?}

Avery pulled at the itchy, thick scarf her mother wrapped her in. "Oui. I left it in the car and Carson brought me to school this morning." {Yes}

According to Avery, her family was the only interesting thing about her, despite its size. They had moved from France when she was a toddler because Southern France wasn't the most inviting place for interracial couples like her parents. Mr and Mrs Toussaint were used to the comments, treatment and looks that came with being together but decided they didn't want their young daughter to grow up in such an environment. Maybe the opinion there had progressed through the years, but the Toussaints had established quite a happy life where they currently lived and wouldn't dream of moving.

Mr Toussaint squinted, "He didn't return you home, that boy?" It had been fifteen years since France but his accent was still as strong as ever. Avery had started to believe that it would never change.

She shook her head, "No, he had football practice. You know how committed he is to it and I didn't want to wait on him."

"Or maybe your cookie senses your twinkling. It's like you knew they'd be here, huh?" her mother teased with a light chuckle. Avery and her father laughed along, knowing her love for chocolate chip cookies. Mrs Toussaint's eyes shone with sympathy afterwards, "Well, unfortunately, you won't be getting any tonight. You can't have dairy when you're sick."

Avery's eyes widened, feeling betrayed by her own mother who claimed to love her.

"Papa dites quelquechose," she pleaded with her father to change her mother's mind. She was aware of her father's soft spot for her and pulled her 'puppy' face by widening her eyes and pouting her lips. {Dad, say something}

He stared at her and tried hard to resist.

They stared at each other. Her pleading, and he fighting.

After what felt like five minutes, but was really five seconds, he sighed in defeat and looked at his wife, "Mon ange, just one? You know her love for them." {My angel}

"Philippe, you know dairy leads to mucus and with her track record of being sick-"

He pulled his 'puppy' face at her. Looking at both her daughter and her husband pouting at her, she could see the obvious similarities between them. She rolled her eyes, giving in out of annoyance, "Just one- the smallest one from the batch. Do you hear me, Avery Toussaint?"

Avery grinned in victory without a response, knowing she was going to take more than that.

****

Avery decided to drive to school today. She had given Carson an earful over the phone last night while knowing he wasn't completely to be blamed. He was simply doing her a favour when he offered to drive her to school and he had only hoped she would stay behind to watch him practice. That's the kind of person he was anyway- considerate and caring.

As she carefully pulled into the school parking lot, she could spot her best friend standing up anxiously, waiting for her. When she parked and stepped out of the car, Carson ran up to her with worry etched on his features.

He ran his hand through his dark and tousled hair, "Are you really sick? When you told me you were actually coming to school I thought it wasn't that bad but, look at you, your nose is all pink." He felt her forehead and continued rambling, "I really didn't mind taking you home yesterday. I just thought you would want to watch me practice."

Avery slapped his hand away, sniffling. "Good morning to you too," she mumbled, "Watching you practice sounds exciting and all, but I'm not really interested in watching people kick around a ball."

He ignored her playful jab towards the sport that defined his life and together, they walked towards the school building, Carson sending worrisome looks to Avery every now and then. She sneezed violently and felt her whole world shake. The intensity of the sneeze was so high she instantly felt disoriented.

"Should you even be here? You never come to school when you're sick," Carson handed her a tissue from his bag. She took it with while muttering a 'thank you'.

"Maman forced me because-"

Avery's sentence was interrupted by one of Carson's football friends calling to him in the corridor.

"Sorry Aves, I'll catch up to you in a bit, okay? Don't die while I'm gone," he rushed over to the other boy, and they both erupted into an animated conversation.

Avery kept walking. She was used to things like this happening. Carson was significantly more popular than her, not that she minded. She preferred not being noticed. Why would she be anyway? She wasn't apart of any special sport or clique. She didn't go to school in fabulous clothes and heels, she put effort into her outfits but, not a lot. Just enough to blend in. She also didn't engage in drama or have relationships.

The school population was too big for her to be well-known without reason. Her main best friend was Carson and she had the occasional acquaintance in each of her classes, but that was good enough for her.

Avery's thoughts drowned out the noisy hallway as she made her way to her locker. Classes were about to start, so the corridors were crowded with the hustle and bustle of students. During this time it was expected to brush a couple of shoulders here and there with different students, but what she didn't expect was to roughly bump into another person.

This snapped her out of her mind and her body switched off its autopilot as she looked up at the taller girl in front of her. When the realization set in that the person looking down at her with a scowl on her face was none other than Alex Rivers surrounded by her small group of very intimidating friends, her body tensed.

"Can you watch where you're going?" Alex glared. Avery was struggling to find her voice and her eyes shifted from the floor and back to brunette, nervously.

"Cat got your tongue?" Alex smirked at the shorter girl's silence. Her smirk was soon replaced with disgust when Avery opened her mouth to respond, but let out a sneeze instead.

On her.

On Alex.

When Avery looked back up and noticed what she had just done, she froze.

She got spit on Alex Rivers in front of a whole crowd of students who had stopped to observe the altercation.

So much for not dying.

Chapter 2

A lex observed the smaller girl who seemed to be rooted in her spot. After she had gotten over the shock, and frankly disgust, of being sneezed on, she allowed to her eyes to fully take Avery in. She analyzed her from her messy bun of chocolate brown curls, her soft freckles dotting her nose and cheeks to the way how her frame almost seemed to tremble with fright as Alex looked on at her.

"Hm," Alex hummed before she brushed past Avery, her friends following in tow. The group walked away with an admirable amount of coordination.

Avery let out a sigh of relief as she watched Alex's retreating figure, her body instantly relaxing. She couldn't help but send up a silent prayer that the situation didn't go as poorly as it could have. Given her reputation, Alex Rivers was not someone that was to be messed with especially not when she was with her friends. Avery couldn't even fight a piece of paper, much less her.

She could only hope that Alex and her fellow school mates (those who gathered to watch the altercation) would forget that this had happened and she would never have to hear about nor think about it again.

She knew that for them to forget it would have to be a miracle, but that didn't stop her from hoping. And boy, did she hope as her feet stayed rooted to the floor and she screwed her eyes shut to let in a few deep breaths.

The weight of her embarrassment lightened as the school bell rang, signalling it was time for everyone get to their first class. The students who were once crowded around her scurried off to go to their individual class-rooms, giving her space to breathe. She was never a fan of crowded areas.

Once everyone was gone, Avery could finally move again and she walked briskly to her locker where she saw Carson leaning against it. She put her hand to her forehead as she tried to calm down from the rush of anxiety that situation had just given her.

"What did I tell you about not dying while I was gone?" Carson joked, standing up correctly. His locker, coin-cidentally, was right next to hers. After he opened it, he presented her with a box of tissues. "I think these will come in handy for next time," he winked before chuckling.

Avery felt her cheeks flare and she held her head down. She groaned, "Carson, I can't believe I did that."

After she had gathered her books from her locker, he swung his arm over her shoulder. His fingers caressed it lightly in an expression of comfort as he led her to their class.

"Hey, don't worry about it too much," he attempted to reassure her, "Give it a few hours and everyone will move on to the next piece of drama."

When they reached their classroom and Carson had opened the door, Avery's anxiety sky-rocketed as the eyes of her peers in her Calculus II class seem to shift to her position. Carson gave her shoulder a reassuring squeeze before they parted ways and went to their separate desks. It was Avery's idea at the start of the term that they should sit far away from each other, so as not to distract themselves but she was starting to regret that now. Her anxiety and the occurrences of merely just 5 minutes ago, left her feeling embarrassed and isolated.

Avery opened her notebook and tried her best to follow along with the class.

****

To say Alex was thrown off-guard would be an understatement. Never had she encountered someone with the audacity to bump into her, much less sneeze on her. Sure, Alex had a feeling that it took the freckled girl a while to recognise just exactly who she was when she had bumped into her, but that thought put her off even more.

After spending the last few minutes in the bathroom, wiping herself off with tissue and hand sanitizer, Alex went to rejoin her friends in their special area.

Their special area was a small classroom in an abandoned block of the school campus. Since the school was so big, no teachers had thought (or cared) to check there for delinquent students who may be skipping classes. It was an unspoken rule throughout the student body that Alex and her crew had marked that block as their territory and anyone who dared to tell administration would face the consequences.

"Surprisingly, Freckles didn't leave that much snot behind," Alex commented to her friends.

"Why the fuck would you tell us that, Lex," Kaden wrinkled his nose in disgust before taking a drag from the spliff he lit.

"Oh, sorry I didn't realise that hearing about the event would be more traumatising than being a victim to the event," Alex bit back, grabbing the spliff from Kaden.

Jason scoffed at the two's antics, playing with his switchblade. His legs were perched on a desk as he rocked back and forth in his chair. He had never been one for much words. He was tall and muscular and had a knack for intimidating people with his build and silence.

"Why call her 'Freckles'?" Sam asked, "Hers aren't even that prominent. I hardly think it's a feature that's worth a nickname."

"Because," Alex started, flicking Kaden on the back of the head to annoy him, "It's unique. I've never seen freckles on a brown girl before."

"Woah, is it even okay to call her that?" Kaden asked, looking at Sam.

"Kaden stop looking at me because I'm the only black person in the room," Sam rolled his eyes. He shifted towards Alex, "I get what you mean. It's not every day you see freckles on a brown girl."

"You guys are talking way too much right now," Jason gruffed.

"Calm down, Grumpy Pants," Kaden retorted, rolling his eyes. In the blink of an eye, Jason was holding Kaden by the hair with a blade to his neck.

"Okay, okay, okay," Kaden repeated with his hands up, surrendering. Jason tightened his hold on him and growled, before shoving him off. Though he was also kind of built (and kind of slow), Kaden knew that he was no match for Jason.

The bell in the small classroom rang, announcing it was time for the next class.

Alex got up from her chair and grabbed her bag, "Well boys, it was nice spending first period with you but I gotta bounce."

"You don't have to," Sam replied, "You just know you have the same free period as Freckles right now and you probably want to intimidate her."

Alex smirked at him, "What can I say? I'm a predictable gal."

Chapter 3

A very normally spent her free periods in the library where she could bury herself in dozens of books. Unfortunately, Carson didn't share the same free period as her so she didn't really have anyone that she wanted to talk to. The other students normally went outside of the building or off campus for their free. That included some of her random acquaintances.

"Hey Freckles," she heard a slightly unfamiliar voice. Not lifting her eyes from her book, she ignored it. Why don't people understand that a library is a place for peace and quiet? Okay, maybe that was a bit hypocritical of her to think that as she had been sniffling the whole time she was there.

"Freckles," the voice sounded again.

Suddenly, a hand slammed loudly on her table. The sound seemed to echo throughout the entire room. Avery jumped in her seat, "Mon Dieu." Her book fell from her hands and landed on the table. When she looked up, she stared right into the eyes of Alex Rivers.

"Hi," Alex smiled, sickeningly sweet before taking a seat across from Avery.

"Hi..." Avery responded hesitantly, feeling very unsettled. She shifted in her seat before looking down at the table, instantly finding the design of the wood very interesting. She expected Alex to start cursing her off or threatening to fight her or anything along those lines really. What she didn't expect was for her to continue staring at her.

Maybe what she wanted was an apology. Avery opened her mouth, struggling to find the words at first.

"L-listen, I'm honestly so sorry for what happened this morning before first period. I never meant to sneeze on you, I've just been battling this wicked cold since yesterday. You see, I was walking home in the rain after school because I left my car at home. I don't normally leave my car at home, but my best friend Carson offered to give me a ride. Well, you see he has football practice after school and I-," the words just seemed to spew out of Avery's mouth like she was a human water fountain.

Alex cocked an eyebrow as she continued to stare at her, finding the situation very amusing.

"-didn't want to wait for him to finish and... please don't hurt me."

Alex chuckled while running a hand through her black hair, "Yeah, okay. Sounds like a wild story. I'll let you off the hook."

"Really?" Avery's eyes brightened. "Just like that?"

"Hm," Alex seemed to think about it, pursing her lips. "No."

"No?" Avery felt so anxious that she could start hyper-ventilating at any minute. She wasn't used to any sort of confrontation like this. Her life was so normal and she was never the centre of attention. She was used to floating by unnoticed; the perfect wallflower.

"Yeah, no," she smirked while getting up from the table. Avery hoped it was because she was getting ready to leave and not to fight her.

Her silent prayers were answered. Alex grabbed her bag from the back of the chair and slung it over her shoulder. Before leaving, she leaned in and said, "Because I was never going to hurt you anyway."

****

Avery groaned to her best friend, "Carson, it was absolutely terrible. I felt like I was going to die."

Carson looked up at Avery over his food. Feeling guilty for letting her walk home the day before, he treated her out to a diner after school.

"But, didn't you say she said that she wasn't going to hurt you?"

Avery sneezed, evoking a "dude, not on my fries" from Carson. "Yeah, but you should've been there. She was all intimidating. She slammed her hand down on the table for starters."

"And?"

"And she kept staring at me."

Carson started to laugh, causing a deep frown to settle on Avery's face. How could her best friend laugh at something like this? What kind of best friend was he?

"It's not funny, I was anxious and uncomfortable," she huffed, crossing her arms like a little girl throwing a temper tantrum.

"Okay, tell you what," Carson said, taking a breath, "Kaden Aldridge is throwing a party on Saturday. Why don't we go and relieve some of your anxiety?"

Avery and parties didn't go well together. The only time you'd hear 'Avery' and 'party' in the same sentence is when the words 'didn't go to the' were in between them.

"Do you even know me?" Avery deadpanned, "Going to a party will increase my anxiety, which I think is the opposite effect you're going for."

Carson was unsure of what else to offer. He and Avery were polar opposites. They were such an odd pairing, people often wondered how they had ended up as best friends. If you were to ask them, they wouldn't really know what to tell you. According to them, they just met and they hit it off. Despite their differences, both Carson and Avery would never wish for another best friend.

"I really don't know what to tell you, Aves. It would mean a lot to me if you came. You never go to parties." Carson pleaded with her, "I'll make sure you have fun."

Avery was sceptical but seeing the look on Carson's face and the way his big blue eyes seemed to get even bigger as he begged her, she reluctantly gave in.

"I can't promise I'll be there because I have to ask maman and papa but, we'll see."

Carson reached over the table to give Avery a big hug, accidentally spilling her frozen lemonade. "Merde. Carson," Avery groaned as she felt a chunk of slush from the cold drink drip from the table and land on her exposed thigh. She grabbed a couple of napkins from the holder at their table and started wiping it off. {Shit}

Carson looked at her sheepishly before he helped her clean up. Avery was just ready to go home, she had had enough of everything and everyone for the day.

****

As she opened the front door to her house, Avery's mind went to the batch of cookies her maman had made yesterday afternoon. There was still a lot left considering

Avery had only had one of them after dinner. Normally when her maman makes cookies, they'd be finished within the next 24 hours.

She silently closed the door and carefully took off her shoes by the welcome mat. She wondered to herself if she should call for her parents like she usually does when she returns home from school and she silently prayed that her mother wasn't at home.

Before she could finish making her decision, she heard footsteps coming down the stairs. She tensed as she was already on her way to the kitchen. If it was her mother she could pretend like she was just getting some orange juice from the fridge. Of course, orange juice! Her mom would love that. She'd go on saying orange juice has the right vitamins to treat her cold. Speaking of which, Avery's body seemed to betray her right then and there as she sneezed violently.

"Avery, c'est toi?" {Is it you?}

Avery's shoulders relaxed as she heard her father's voice. When he finished his descent down the stairs, she smiled at him.

"Oui, papa. It's just me," she responded to him. "Is maman home?"

Mr Toussaint gave his daughter a knowing look. "Non, what is it that you want? The cookies?"

Avery chuckled nervously, "Would you tell maman if I said yes?"

"Ah, I would not. Mais ta mère, well she hid them from you." {But your mother,}

"Where?" Avery pouted. Her father pointed to a cupboard that could be seen through the opening in the wall of the kitchen that created their breakfast bar.

"L'arrière," he said, telling her that the cookies were hidden at the back of the cupboard. {The back}

"Merci, papa," she kissed her father, preparing to run into the kitchen and raid the cookie jar. Before she ran off she hesitated, remembering Carson. {Thanks, dad}

"Papa... there's a party at this guy's house that's happening on Saturday. Carson asked me if I wanted to go and I said I'd ask. So, can I go?"

"Une fête?" {A party?}

"Oui, je sais. But everything will be fine, I'd be going with Carson." {Yes, I know}

"Who is 'this guy'?" her father asked her.

"His name is Kaden Aldridge, he's Carson's friend," Avery responded. In truth, she didn't even know who Kaden Aldridge was, but her father didn't know that. Plus, Carson was friends with, well, everybody.

"Ah, Carson's friend. C'est un homme bon. Sure, you can go. I'll tell your maman when she gets home," her father smiled, secretly happy his daughter was going out and being an eighteen year old. {That's a good man}

Avery smiled back at him before heading towards the kitchen.

Her maman was good at lots of things, but probably the only thing she wasn't good at was hiding stuff. When Avery opened the cupboard her father had directed her to, she spotted the lid of the cookie jar behind some containers of seasonings.

Her face broke out into a grin. Jackpot.

Chapter 4

Saturday came as quickly as it could as if the universe was in a rush to make Avery's life a living hell.

It was only one in the afternoon and Avery sat on the carpet in her walk-in closet, considering what to wear. She had chosen five different outfits which she had placed neatly on her bed for further critique, but there was a nagging feeling that she hadn't picked the best ones.

What should she even wear to the party? Was it a casual party? Semi-formal, maybe? Should she wear a romper? A dress? Jeans and a blouse? Should she dress simply to blend in, or would dressing simply make her stand out?

Avery frustratedly ran a hand through her dishevelled curls and let out a deep sigh. Her room, along with her closet, was painted mint-green, her calm colour. But, not even that or the smell of her mother baking a fresh batch of cookies (after Avery had accidentally finished the old batch in the jar on Wednesday), could lessen her anxiety as she dreaded the party.

It was no secret that Avery suffered from general anxiety. She was diagnosed, five years ago at thirteen years old and once she and her parents had discovered that mint-green seemed to help, almost everything she owned was decorated with the colour. It was an unconventional method, but it had always helped.

With another huff, Avery changed from her seated position as she uncrossed her legs to lay down on the fluffy carpet. She ran her fingers up and down the carpet, finding comfort in its soft feel.

"Avery," Mrs Toussaint called out as she entered her daughter's room, carrying a plate of chocolate chip cookies with her. She looked around and gasped when she spotted her daughter's form on the floor of her closet. She gently placed the plate on the dresser before rushing over to Avery.

"Doux-Doux, ça va? Qu'est-ce qui ne va pas?" she sat down next to Avery's lying form, and gingerly rested Avery's head on her lap. {Sweetie, what's going on? What's wrong?}

"Ça va, maman. C'est la fête ce soir. Je n'ai rien à porter," Avery sighed to her mother. {I'm okay, mom. It's the party tonight. I don't have anything to wear}

"Ah, but you have plenty to wear," Mrs Toussaint gestured to the racks of clothing in front of them. "T'as beaucoup de vêtements but you just wear the same things over and over." {You have lots of clothes}

"Can you help me pick something out then?" Avery asked.

"Mais, bien sûr!" she squeezed her daughter's cheeks together before they both stood up. {But, of course!}

Forty-five minutes to an hour later, they had both finally agreed on an outfit for Avery to wear to the party. It was a flowing black crop top with long sleeves, a white pair of high-waisted shorts accompanied by black wedged booties. The women stood proudly over their decision which was laid out neatly on Avery's bed.

" Génial! You can pick up any young man in this," her mother teased before grabbing a cookie off of the plate and biting into it. {Great!}

"Maman!" Avery blushed heavily, folding her arms in embarrassment.

"Maybe even Carson. I wouldn't be surprised if that boy was totally head over heels for you," Mrs Toussaint continued, causing Avery to cover her face with her hands.

"Nous sommes seulement amis, maman," Avery mumbled behind her hands. {We're only friends, mom}

"Les amis, les amoureux... same thing," Her mother said in a sing-song voice before exiting her room. {Friends, lovers}

****

Carson pulled up to Avery's house at eight o' clock on the dot, just like he had promised her. Avery felt her hands tremble and she stuffed them in the back pockets of her shorts to get her mind off of them. She instead decided to focus on what a beautiful night it was, it was peaceful and quiet.

Tonight was a full moon and the milky white sphere was only partially covered by light wisps of clouds. The light from the moon created a ring of colours, hues of orange and blue that reflected onto the clouds and made a beautiful outline.

"-very," someone called out to her. Avery's head snapped to the direction of the sound to find Carson patiently waiting for her. He was leaned against his car wearing a white button-up shirt that defined his muscles which he gained from football.

The right football. Not what the Americans called 'soccer'. American football was just a fancy way of saying rugby. Avery wrinkled her face in annoyance as she got lost in her thoughts. It's like America decided to call rugby 'football' so they obviously couldn't call football 'football' because they had already dubbed rugby that name, so they went ahead and called it 'soccer'. It was so confusing and unnecessary. In French, football was football, and French was her first language. It was frustrating to learn that certain places called football 'football' or football 'soccer'. How could she ever know which one was which?

Carson was the type of person who dressed to impress, he dressed almost always formally for every occasion. Even for something as insignificant as school. With that, his chivalry and his good looks, there was no wonder why he had so many girls chasing after him. He maybe even had a few guys.

Snapping out of her thoughts, Avery walked towards the car and got in hesitantly.

"How are you feeling?" Carson asked her, he turned to face her in the car while putting his hand on the back of her seat. He gave her a reassuring smile.

"I'll be fine, let's just go," she responded to him, sending him a smile of her own. Carson pursed his lips in thought before twisting to the steering wheel and placing the key in the ignition. Soon, they were on their way.

Avery had no doubt in her mind that she would hate this experience. As they stood on the lawn of the large house, she could feel the bass of the loud music vibrating in her organs. Red cups and drunk teenagers seemed to be everywhere. Couldn't Kaden have been the person to break the stereotype and just use blue cups? Maybe green? The trope of having red cups at a party was so overdone.

It had been less than a minute and Avery just wanted to run back home, but when Carson asked her if she was ready to go in she just smiled and nodded, looping their arms together. A surge of confidence ran through her as she walked in with her best friend, but it left as quickly as it came.

"I know it seems a bit overwhelming, Aves," Carson reassured her, his voice raising to combat the volume of their surroundings. "You'll get used to it after a while. Let me introduce you to Kaden...if we can find him."

Kaden Aldridge wasn't hard to find. He stood with a group of three other people, one of which Avery recognised as Alex Rivers. She didn't recognise the others, but she felt intimidated by all four of them. Her reflexes kicked in and she slightly stepped behind Carson, wishing she could be invisible as they seemed to watch her and Carson as they both got closer to their group.

Carson confidently strode over to them, gracefully making his way through the crowd of different sweaty bodies. Avery could feel herself going through sensory overload as she followed him.

"Hey, Aldridge!" Carson called out to him. Kaden smiled. He put down his beer bottle and swung himself off of the counter which he was previously seated on. Avery watched awkwardly as Carson and Kaden gave each other some weird 'bro handshake' and embrace.

"Yo," Kaden said, dragging out the ending. He shouted out over the music, to whoever could hear, "Hey every-one! Number Five is here!"

The crowd of teenagers cheered and some even raised their cups and bottles, celebrating the arrival of Carson 'Number Five' Armani. Saying Avery felt out of place would be an understatement. As she watched Carson shake hands with and hug all the people who came up to greet him, she was reminded once more that this was not her scene. Carson, when he was 'Number Five', was so different from the Carson she knew when they were alone. He was more outgoing and seemed to be in his element.

Avery sighed, looking for somewhere silent she could sit and ride out the party. Carson may have been with her now, but give it a moment and he would be whisked away from her side. While he was chatting with some friends, he made eye contact with her and sent her an apologetic smile. "I'll come to find you later," he mouthed to her. Looks like that moment was now.

What had felt like hours but had only been thirty minutes later, Avery found a place on the porch she could sit where it seemed a little quieter than the chaos going on inside and on the front lawn. Somehow she had ended up with a red cup In her hand and glitter in her hair. 'Maybe booties weren't the best thing to wear to a party,' Avery thought to herself as she slipped them off, laying them on the floor before gently massaging the soles of her feet.

The abundance of people at the party was overwhelming. Though it was a large house, the school population was even larger and everyone seemed to know Kaden Aldridge. Or maybe they didn't know him all that well, and they were just there for a party. Avery felt humid, sticky and sweaty and hated the feeling that came from having people's damp skin all over hers. Whatever the beverage was in her hand felt cool and she went to take a sip from it. It was kind of sweet but with a bitter aftertaste. It left a weird feeling in Avery's chest as it went down and she made up her face in dislike at the sensation. But overall, the drink didn't taste so bad and so she went to sip again.

"You probably shouldn't be drinking that," Avery heard a voice call out. She hesitated as the cup was to her lips, then realised the person may have been talking to someone else and continued.

While she was in the process of finishing the contents in the red cup, she felt the presence of someone shadowing over her. She looked up to find Alex Rivers there, looking down at her with a frown. Alex took the cup from her grasp.

"Um, excuse me?" Avery said in annoyance. She halted. Where did that confidence come from? Alex looked unfazed by the response from the freckled girl as she poured out the remaining liquid from the cup.

"Where did you get this?" Alex asked her, folding her arms after she let the cup fall to the floor. Avery frowned at the blatant pollution. "I'm not sure," she drew her eyebrows together in confusion, "Someone must've given it to me."

Alex scoffed in annoyance, "People put all sorts of crap into drinks at parties. You don't just take drinks from anybody. Where's Carson?"

Avery shrugged, brushing her feet along the wooden floor as she looked down. She was starting to feel dizzy. Alex narrowed her eyes at Avery, "You better hope there was nothing dangerous in this drink."

Avery was surprised and confused about why Alex seemed to care about her wellbeing. They had only just met this week and spoken twice if one would even call their encounters conversations. From what she had heard and gathered, Alex didn't seem like that kind of person. Avery voiced her confusion, "Why do you care?"

"I care because too much bad shit happens to naive little girls at house parties," Alex bit out. She may not have known Avery personally but she had at least hoped that she had more sense than to drink suspicious liquid given to her by a stranger. Her features softened as she saw how lost and out of place Avery looked. She muttered a string of curses under her breath at the feeling that tugged at her chest and held out her hand to Avery.

Avery looked up at Alex, confusion written in her facial features as she shifted her focus to the arm that was stretched out to her. She felt herself get dizzier and brushed some imaginary curls from her face. Her hair was in a neatly made bun on top of her head, but for some reason, she felt like they were out and wild.

She took Alex's hand after a moment and felt the taller girl pull her back into the house. They weaved through the cluster of bodies and Avery cringed to herself. She didn't think twice when Alex brought her up a flight of stairs, she had just wanted to escape the chaos that was going on.

After walking for a while and going around some corners, Alex opened a door to a room. It was too dark for Avery too see inside and her adrenaline spiked. She felt panic nipping at her chest and she gasped. What was happening?

She felt her chest rising up and down at an increasing rate. She squeezed her eyes shut before opening them again. She was almost heaving when Alex flipped on the light switch, "This is my room- hey are you okay?" She was now facing Avery in concern. She guided her to the bed and sat her down.

"I'm fine," Avery said between breaths, willing herself to calm down. 'Look for something green, look for something green,' Avery repeated to herself in her mind as her eyes flicked to every surface in the room in a frenzy.

"I figured you'd want somewhere to stay to ride out whatever was in that cup. I can keep the door locked and go back downstairs if you want. Every time there's a party here, everyone knows this room is out of bounds so no one comes in here really," Alex rubbed her back, trying to soothe her.

Avery snapped her eyes back to Alex to find the taller girl looking at her with deep concern evident in her own. Alex's green eyes seemed to sedate Avery's anxiety and she took slow breaths as she continued to stare into them. In their two encounters, Avery had never noticed that Alex had green eyes. She also never noticed the flecks of gold that almost seemed to dance close to her pupil.

And then and there, she felt totally calm staring into Alex's eyes.

"Are you okay?" Alex asked once more, hoping to snap the freckled girl out of the trance she seemed to be in. She didn't know what to do and had started to panic herself.

"Um, yeah," Avery said slowly, looking down. She noticed that at some point, Alex had gripped her hand so she let go and moved away from Alex on the bed, praying it was subtle and that she wouldn't take offence. "You said this was your room, right? Isn't this Kaden Aldridge's house?"

Alex chuckled and she got up, feeling relieved that Avery seemed to be okay now. "Kaden is my step-brother so yeah, I live here."

"Oh," Avery responded softly, her eyes roaming the room carefully. When she had been scanning the place for something green, she never stopped to take in what it was like. At first glance, she wouldn't have guessed it was Alex's room. The room was minimalist, its walls were a light beige and everything else had either light

grey or eggshell white accents. There wasn't much dec-
orating the walls except for a few family photographs
and paintings. It didn't feel homely at all. Avery frowned
at that, there was no way to tell who Alex was or that
she even lived here.

Alex followed Avery's gaze and seemed to realise what
she was thinking, "I haven't really gotten around to dec-
orating."

Avery looked back at her. She was wearing a dark
green leather jacket, plain white shirt, black jeans and
black combat boots. Who was Alex Rivers? "How long
have you lived here?" she asked.

Alex seemed to think about it, "Um, my mom married
Kaden's dad about two years ago. So, yeah."

Avery narrowed her eyes, "Okay." Another wave of
dizziness hit her and she felt like she was staggering
backwards even though she was firmly planted on the
bed. She groaned and held her forehead with her hands,
"I just recovered from a cold, and now this?" She flopped
down onto the bed to a lying position and the movement made her feel as if she was falling into another
dimension. "Am I drunk? Is this what being drunk feels
like?"

Alex smirked, creating an unsettling feeling in Avery's
stomach, "Possibly. Is this the first you've drunk, Freckles?"

"Avery. My name is Avery," Avery muttered, "Yeah, it is."

"Well, I'm glad I was here to witness your first time," Alex commented, walking over to a loveseat that was positioned not so far away from the bed. She sat down, positioning her body so that her legs could dangle over the armrest.

"Well, what do I do now?" Avery felt her words become more sluggish, she rolled over to lie on her side so she could continue looking at Alex as they spoke.

"You can either join the party downstairs or sleep up here until it goes away."

Avery wrinkled her nose as soon as she heard the words 'join the party' and she yawned. "I'd rather just stay up here if it's not too much trouble," Avery said.

Alex nodded before Avery started to continue, "Just tell Carson where I am if you see him at any point, please. He's my ride home and he'll probably be worried about me."

That was what she had meant to say but at that point, when it had left her mouth it was incoherent and her words sounded all mushed together. Alex observed as her eyes began to flutter and Avery's head nestled its way in the crook of her own arm.

Alex smiled softly at the freckled girl. Feeling cozy in her loveseat, she took her phone out from her pocket and started playing a game. It wasn't a conscious decision because she had planned to go back downstairs to party with Kaden, Sam and Jason, but she ended up spending the whole night in the room, just to make sure Freckles would be okay.

Chapter 5

It was now the middle of autumn and Avery was more than excited. Today she had planned to go for a walk along her favourite walking trail. It was always beautiful this time of year, covered with brown, yellow, red and orange leaves. She would always return home with crushed foliage in her hair because she was never able to resist the urge to jump into a pile of leaves and start making angels in them.

She was in the process of putting on her cardigan and boots when her phone rang, vibrating in the back pocket of her jeans. A picture she had taken of herself and Carson presented itself on the screen of her phone when she took it out.

The party at Kaden's house had taken place two weeks ago and Carson had been upset at her the following day. At first, Avery had felt guilty when he told her about how worried he was and the lengths he went to just to find out she was okay and sleeping upstairs. But after a while, she didn't feel guilty when she remembered that it was Carson who had left her in the first place and she would've had an anxiety attack if it wasn't for Alex Rivers. So she stated her claim and the tables turned.

Avery's finger swiped the screen to accept the call. "Hey Aves, are you on your way?" Carson's voice sounded through the speaker. The phone was now nestled in the crook between her jaw and her shoulder as she bent down, tying the laces of her boots while folding her lips in concentration. She hummed affirmatively and said, "Yeah, I should be there in two minutes or so."

For once, Carson didn't seem to have football practice on a Saturday and was able to join Avery on her walk to admire the beauty of autumn. When she finished getting ready, Avery called out a goodbye to her parents before leaving the house.

The chilly wind greeted her as soon as she stepped outside and it ruffled her curls. A small smile settled on her face as she took a deep breath in and started down the pavement to the point where she and Carson were meant to meet. Upon seeing her best friend dressed in a sweatshirt, joggers and sneakers, she knew they were both on this walk for different reasons. He was obviously going to jog (most likely run) in compensation for his cancelled football practice.

"You have a problem," she rolled her eyes at him when she reached him. Carson was stretching and bouncing on the balls of his feet, warming himself up for his run. He paused for a while to give Avery a friendly hug. "You just can't give yourself a break, can you?"

Carson chuckled lightly, picking his water bottle up from the ground, "If I want to do this professionally, I can't just be taking breaks whenever I can."

"Well, I won't be jogging with you. I'm here for the scenery, not for exercise," Avery folded her arms, slightly whipping her head back to move the hair from her face. Maybe it wasn't the best idea to wear her hair out on such a windy day.

Carson observed Avery's attire, "Really? I never would've guessed." He smirked playfully, bumping his shoulder with hers. Well, his forearm, based on their height difference.

"You look cute though," he added as they both started walking towards the trail, "I might have to fight down a few thirsty boys."

"Oh yeah?" Avery snorted, her words laced with sarcasm, "Hope you can put up a good fight."

Carson shook his head as he laughed before picking up the pace, leaving Avery some way behind him. "Already?" she called out after him in disbelief.

A big gust of wind hit Avery, getting a few strands of hair in her eye. She groaned and halted her slow pace. She may not have been the best at planning ahead, but she always stored spare hair ties in the pockets of her clothing. This time, it came in handy as she bunched up her hair, fixing it into a messy bun. A few stray curls of baby hair fell out at the back, sides and front of her hair despite her attempts to smooth it down. Giving up, she continued on her walk.

She walked slowly down the pavement, her head in the clouds as she admired the trees and the leaves on the ground.

She remembered the first time her parents took her to this pathway to play in the leaves. It was the first of November, exactly eleven years ago when she was seven years old. She was having a bad day, throwing 'fits' at school (which they would later find out was caused by her anxiety) leaving Mrs Toussaint feeling torn. Due to the way she was raised by her Congolese parents, she would have spanked Avery for her bad behaviour as her parents believed that that was the best way for children to learn. They believed that if a child feels negative consequences after they did something wrong, they would be less likely to repeat what they had done. It was what Mrs Toussaint had known.

Avery had disrupted her class multiple times, leaving her teacher frustrated and her classmates upset and so in return, Mrs Toussaint had to discipline her daughter. After she had sat Avery down after school, Avery burst into uncontrollable tears and Mrs Toussaint couldn't find it within herself to hurt her child. She looked to her husband to do the job but in France, they looked down upon corporal punishments. He had been born and raised in France, like his wife, but unlike her, he had French parents, not Congolese ones. Seeing how upset both his daughter and wife were, he suggested they take a walk.

It was during their walk that they stumbled upon the walking trail. Seeing the pretty colours of all the leaves had lifted Avery's spirits and she tugged on her father's hand, pulling him into the area of trees off the side of the pavement to play in them. Despite the day's previous negativities, Avery always regarded it as one of the best days of her life.

Steering off the trail and into the area filled with trees, Avery took out her phone to take pictures. She stooped down the ground, angling herself and placing her phone in the position to get the best picture. She looked down at the screen and smiled to herself in satisfaction.

When Carson jogged back to meet his best friend twenty minutes later, he noticed she was nowhere to be found. "Shit," he cursed under his breath, feeling the same feeling of worry in his chest that he had felt two weeks ago at the party when he couldn't find Avery. It was when he brought his hand up to run it through his hair, he saw movement through a space in the trees. Walking towards it and moving the branches out of his way he found Avery in a pile of leaves that she must have put together herself. A big smile on her face and a couple of leaves in her hair, she looked up and greeted him breathlessly, "Hi! How was your jog?"

He shook his head at her, a small smile playing at his lips, "You scared me, you know?" Reaching out a hand to her, he pulled her up out of the leaf pile and helped dust her off. When they were finished and most of the foliage seemed to be out of her hair and off of her clothes, Carson put his arm over her shoulder, "Want to go to Starbucks?" he asked. Avery smiled and nodded.

Though Carson was more than willing to walk to the café, Avery insisted that it was too far and so the two found themselves walking back to her house so that she could drive her car. After a few short minutes of walking, they reached Avery's house. Her mother had been watering the plants outside and so spotted her daughter and her best friend. She smiled and sent them a wave.

"Bonjour, madame," Carson waved back to Mrs Toussaint. She embraced him, kissing both his cheeks. "Bonjour, Carson. How are you? It's been a while since I've seen you." {Hello, Ma'am}

"Yes, madame. I've been really busy with football. This is my last year of high school and I'm working really hard to get a scholarship."

Both Avery and Mrs Toussaint found it admirable how polite and gentlemanly Carson could be. Avery had always somewhat envied his ability to win the hearts of any crowd.

"Yes, that's what Avery tells me. She speaks highly of how committed you are. Mr Toussaint and I would love it if you could stop by for dinner one day after school?"

"Well, Wednesday is the only day during the week that I don't have practice, so I'll take you up on that offer next Wednesday, madame." Mrs Toussaint nodded appreciatively before turning to her daughter, "So, what are you kids doing here so soon?"

"Nous allons à Starbucks, maman," Avery responded to her mother. "We only stopped here so I could get the car." {We're going to Starbucks, mom}

"D'accord. Have fun," Mrs Toussaint opened the garage for her daughter using the remote in the pocket of her apron. {Okay}

"À bientôt," Carson said to Avery's mother, bidding her goodbye. Over the years that he and Avery had been friends, he had taken it upon himself to learn a few French phrases and the gesture greatly warmed the family's hearts. Mr and Mrs Toussaint primarily speak English when they are around him in order to make him feel included, so it really was not necessary. {See you later}

Avery grabbed her car keys from a bowl that was perched on a desk in the garage. After they got in Carson commented to her, "You know I really love your mom."

"Yeah well, she really loves you too. It's because she thinks you were raised well and are the perfect gentle-man. It also helps that she thinks you're in love with me," Avery giggled slightly with a slight blush.

Carson felt a blush rise to his cheeks as well and moved his head to look out his window as Avery reversed out of the garage. "Well..."

"Oh, don't tell me you're in love with me Carson Armani," Avery teased him, removing one hand from the steering wheel to shove his arm playfully.

Carson paused. "I am," he said, causing Avery to glance over at him, her eyebrows furrowed in confusion and slight guilt.

"I-what?" she whispered.

Suddenly Carson burst out into laughter, unable to keep it in any longer, "Oh my God, you should've seen your face."

"You morceau de merde!" she exclaimed, slapping his arm with her free hand repeatedly while trying to keep her eyes on the road. He grabbed it and gave her palm a small platonic kiss in apology. {piece of shit}

"You suck," Avery groaned, "Don't put me in that situation ever again. I didn't even know what to say. I was so afraid I would hurt your feelings and then things would be awkward."

"I'm sorry, I'm sorry," Carson apologised, "But, I guess I can see why your mom would think that. We are very close friends."

Avery parked her car and the two got out, walking towards the entrance of the Starbucks. "For the distress that you put me through, you're paying for my drink."

Carson swung his arm over her shoulder and rubbed her arm as she pouted. "I'm guessing you want a matcha green tea frappuccino?"

"Yes, please," she smiled.

Carson nodded, moving to join line. Avery decided that she would save them a table so they'd have somewhere to sit when Carson got their drinks. She scanned the room and when she saw an empty booth she walked towards it. She felt her phone vibrate repeatedly in her back pocket as her phone instantly connected to the Wi-Fi. You know what they say, home is where the Wi-Fi connects.

Reaching for her back pocket, she obtained her phone and opened it to check her messages. Her checking was abruptly interrupted by her phone falling to the floor as she bumped into a body. She felt her eyes widen and relief flooded her when she realised the screen had not cracked.

"Wow, Freckles. Fancy that," she heard a familiar voice and a familiar nickname. Standing up with her phone in hand, she faced the source. It was Alex Rivers. The two hadn't seen each other since the party two weeks ago, not that they'd have any reason to. They both took different classes, only sharing a few free periods which they spent in different places. Given the large population of their school as well, there was a low chance that they would bump into each other by accident like their first encounter.

"You know, one time is a mistake but the second time is a decision," Alex smirked teasingly.

Chapter 6

- -

Avery's nose wrinkled, her features express-ing confusion at Alex's statement. "I'm not sure I understand," she said, her tone sounding it out as if it was a question.

"It just kind of feels like you're bumping into me on purpose at this point," Alex shrugged teasingly while using a finger to twirl the end of her hair, pretending to be nonchalant. Avery couldn't help but notice how nicely the messy side braid she sported seemed to com-plement her face. There was no doubt that Alex was insanely attractive. For some reason, Avery blushed at both Alex's comment and her thoughts about Alex's appearance.

"I really didn't mean to. I didn't see you both times I swear," Avery fiddled with her fingers now that she had put her phone back in her pocket. Her blush subsided as her embarrassment turned into nervousness. Alex's smirk only widened to a smile that vanished as quickly as it came as she found herself amused by the shorter girl.

"Where are you headed?" Alex asked. Avery's attention was drawn to the small paper bag Alex was holding for just a second, letting curiosity fill her.

"I was just going to that booth there." Avery pointed to the booth behind Alex which her made the taller girl turn around to see it.

"Did you come alone?"

"No."

After a few moments of awkward silence, Avery realised that Alex was looking for her to elaborate. "I came with Carson."

"Cool. Mind if I sit with you guys for a while?"

The question stunned Avery, "Uh, s-sure. Carson won't mind at all." She paused, "And I wouldn't mind either."

"Okay."

When Carson scanned the room and spotted his friend, he was surprised (more confused) to see a person with seemingly long dark hair sitting next to her in their booth. He was at too far away of a distance to make out the face of who it was, but he knew all of Avery's acquaintances well enough to know that none of them had dark hair.

When he got to the booth and the mysterious dark-haired girl looked up, his confusion turned to shock when he found it was Alex.

"Hey, Alex," he smiled, receiving a small nod of acknowledgement from her and a half-hearted wave. "Here you go, Aves," he placed her green drink in front of her. Avery's eyes brightened as she received her drink and eagerly picked up her straw.

"Paper?" she asked Carson, making sure he had requested a paper straw rather than a plastic one. He nodded and she grinned, unwrapping it and placing it in her drink. She sighed happily after taking a sip, instantly forgetting her nerves that came from sitting next to Alex.

She drank her frappuccino as Alex and Carson started to converse, only stopping to observe when Alex opened her paper bag and pulled out a chocolate chip cookie. Carson paused in the middle of his sentence when he realised how long Avery had been looking at the cookie while Alex slowly broke off pieces of it and placed them in her mouth. "Uh oh," he chuckled.

Alex raised an eyebrow, following the direction of his gaze to the freckled girl sitting next to her.

"Avery really likes chocolate chip cookies," Carson explained for his best friend.

During her sipping not long ago, Avery had come to the conclusion that the only reason Alex decided to join them was that she liked Carson. It would explain why she asked her to sit with them only when she had mentioned Carson and why she sat next to Avery so she could sit across from him. Plus, Alex had barely spoken to her in the time they waited for Carson to arrive, not that she would have any reason to.

It wouldn't be the first time this had happened. Avery had had to put up with many girls who hung around them to gain Carson's attention, but they never stuck around that long because Carson was never really interested, he was only ever appeasing them to be polite. Carson was skilled at reading people and he knew that the majority of them just wished to date him for his popularity and bragging rights. He was a romantic and refused to hook up with different girls as his other friends did. But Avery couldn't picture Alex as a girl who would get rejected; she looked and acted like she could get whatever it was she wanted.

Avery had a feeling that she'd be seeing more of her.

Alex leaned back to rest her back on the seat while she slouched. She slid the paper bag of cookies towards Avery, "Here, you can have them."

She looked at the green-eyed girl in question, "You don't want them?"

Alex shrugged, "I only bought them because they ran out of macadamia nut and I sure as fuck wasn't gonna buy oatmeal."

Avery smiled shyly, brushing some of her baby hairs out of her face. "Thank you."

When Carson resumed his conversation with Alex, he was quick to notice that every now again Alex would side-glance at Avery to watch her enjoy the cookies.

Avery, on the other hand, was in her own little bubble. She munched away happily at Alex's cookies and took sips of her green drink. She didn't even mind that the two other people were deeply engrossed in their own conversation and that she was left out.

After ten or so minutes, Alex got bored and decided it was time for her to go. She stood up from the booth and slipped on her black denim jacket. Carson had finished his drink and got up as well to go to the restroom, leaving the two girls alone once more.

"Hey," Alex called to Avery. She called again after not soliciting a response from her the first time. "Freckles."

The nickname brought Avery back to reality and her head snapped to the tall girl, "Ouais...je- I mean- yeah?" She had almost forgotten what language to speak in and she felt her cheeks slowly heat up at her mistake. It didn't seem like Alex noticed though as she adjusted the sleeves of her jacket, "I'm leaving now."

"Oh, okay. Bye," Avery waved timidly. The response was not what Avery expected it to be as she was met with Alex's outstretched hand as it held a phone. Alex shook the phone while she held it out to Avery, gesturing for her to take it. Avery got the message and took it hesitantly.

"What's this for?" Avery asked, confused.

Alex made a sound that sounded like a cross between a scoff and a chuckle as she shook her head, smiling a little. "Your number, Freckles."

"O-oh. Um, okay," Avery replied awkwardly before pressing the 'Add new contact' option. She put in her name and typed in the digits before saving it and handing the phone back to Alex.

Avery smirked as she looked at the contact details, before changing something, "If I keep you saved as 'Avery Toussaint' I'm not gonna know who the fuck you are. You're Freckles to me."

"Toussaint," Avery mumbled, correcting her pronunciation.

"What?"

"It's pronounced 'Too-saw' with a soft 'n'," Avery spoke up, "Toussaint."

"What kind of complicated last name is that?"

"It's French," Avery shrugged, playing with her napkin in her lap.

"Hm, interesting." And with that, Alex walked away.

Carson returned soon after, wiping his hands with a hand towel. "I guess Alex is gone," he observed. Avery nodded her head and hummed in agreement.

****

"Hi, Avery. How have you been since we've last seen each other?"

Avery shifted slightly in her position in the comfortable sofa and twiddled with her thumbs. "I've been good," she answered timidly.

"Any recent panic or anxiety attacks?" Dr Rosenburg questioned, hovering a pen over a notepad while he sent a reassuring smile to Avery.

"Um," Avery paused to think about it, "Just a handful. The last anxiety attack was two weeks ago when I went to a party. It's been a while since the last panic attack."

Dr Rosenburg nodded before scribbling on the paper. Avery wondered what he was writing so much of after a few moments of hearing the sound of pen against paper. Avery had been going to Dr Rosenburg for a while now, she expected that the doctor would've known her like the back of his hand. But yet, every month it's like there's a whole new world of notes to write.

"How did you deal with it?"

"I breathed..." Avery flushed at the memory, "And looked at something green."

"That's it?"

Avery nodded, feeling awkward.

"What did you look at that was green?"

Avery really hoped Dr Rosenburg wouldn't ask her that question. The answer was so stupid. Her cheeks were blazing at that point, "Someone's eyes."

"Oh?"

"Yes. A...friend."

Dr Rosenburg's head tilted the side as he placed down his pen. He entwined his fingers and used them to hold up his chin as he leaned forward onto his desk in interest. "Carson?" he asked.

"No. Her name is Alex."

"So her green eyes calmed you down. Am I correct?"

"Yes. I know it's dumb." The doctor shook his head, "Not dumb. Just interesting that breathing exercises and looking into her eyes was enough to calm down an attack."

Avery's cheeks blushed once more and she grabbed a cushion from beside her, noting its mint green colour and she hugged it. Dr Rosenburg made sure to add a couple of green things to his office to make Avery feel more comfortable once she became his patient.

"Is it possible that you have feelings for her?"

Avery shook her head. Dr Rosenburg smiled softly. "Are you attracted to girls Avery?" Noticing her hesitation he continued, "It's okay if you are. This is a safe space and same-sex marriage is legal here and in France too."

Avery shook her head once more, wanting to be swallowed by the soft sofa that instant. Why wasn't the hour up yet? "I've never had a crush on anyone before," she said shyly.

The doctor nodded, "And that's perfectly okay."

He lifted his head from its position on his hands and took up his pen, hovering it over the notepad once more. "So, your first party..."

Chapter 7

Alex sat on top of the lunch table she shared with Sam, Jason and Kaden while taking a swig from her water bottle. The lunch area at the school was located outside of its buildings due to its large population. There were tables and benches littered across the campus where the students could sit, talk with their friends and eat their lunch while appreciating nature at the same time.

Alex and her friends were a little bit tipsy from the vodka that she had brought using her water bottle to disguise it. Kaden rested his head and arms on Alex's lap and let out a burp which caused her to wrinkle her nose.

"Guys, guess what?" Kaden lifted his head slightly, showing off a big grin as he looked between his friends. He was met with silence and an eye-roll from Jason. "Come on guys..." he pleaded.

Sam sighed deeply, taking the bottle from Alex who then went to play a game on her phone. "What?" Sam huffed.

"Alex's full name is Alexia! How girly is that?" Kaden started laughing loudly, causing small chuckles to erupt from his friends. Alex, on the other hand, was not amused as she slapped the side of Kaden's head.

"Shut up. No one ever even calls me that," she hissed at the blond boy in her lap. She glanced at her phone screen, "And you made me lose my fucking game."

Kaden only ignored her, sat up and continued. "Okay so, I was going through drawers and cupboards at home, looking for places to hide my weed so the 'rents couldn't find them, right? And one drawer I opened had in some of our documents and so I took out Alex's passport and that's when I saw it," he turned his head to face his step-sister cheekily, "Alexia Celeste Rivers."

Sam smirked, "Who knew that under all that badass exterior there was a real Disney princess?"

Though the rest of his friends were laughing and having a good time under the influence, the corner of Jason's mouth only twitched upward slightly and stayed there for less than a second. The gang was so used to Jason's stoic expressions and deafening silence that they didn't take it to heart when he didn't laugh at their jokes or add to the conversation. They, along with everyone in the school, just knew not to mess with him.

"Did Long just... smile?" Alex changed the subject to their quiet friend. Jason shrugged while his friends inspected his face for any evidence that Alex was just seeing things.

He tilted his head slightly to the left and jutted his chin out, "Freckles."

At the mention of the pet name, Alex's head turned to the direction that Jason gestured to. Her eyes scanned the students and then laid on the curly-haired girl who was sitting on the grass, legs folded and eating a salad.

Avery usually spent her lunchtimes in a more remote area, but today she gave into Carson and sat where he normally did. The two of them sat on the newly cut grass and ate their lunches. Avery had packed a Caesar salad with a brownie while Carson had pizza delivered to their school gate.

"Are you sure you don't want any?" Carson teased her, waving a slice of Hawaiian pizza in front of her face. He watched her eyes follow it.

"Can you stop? You know I'm on a diet," Avery folded her arms and looked down at her salad. She loved Caesar salads but having a slice of cheesy pizza with ham and pineapple sounded way better than lettuce, croutons and cheese.

"But you have a brownie right there," Carson stated. Avery huffed in annoyance, glaring at her friend before plucking the pizza slice from his fingers.

"I hate you and love you so much," Avery groaned, her words muffled by the pizza in her mouth. Carson knew Hawaiian was her favourite. He smiled widely at his friend and ruffled her hair. Avery swallowed before she gasped at his actions. She dropped the pizza slice in her salad bowl to free her hands so she could pry Carson's fingers from her hair. "You can't do that! You don't even know how long it took to perfect these curls this morning. Today was wash day."

Carson only grinned and wrapped his muscular arms around his friend in a tight hug. Avery felt her phone buzz in her front pocket and took it out once Carson let go of her.

Unknown Number: Bonjuor

Avery brought her eyebrows together in confusion at the text before typing back a response.

A: Bonjour. Qu'est-ce? {Hello. Who is this?}

Unknown Number: Slow down Freckles

Unknown Number: I don't know that much french.

Avery turned to Carson. "I think Alex Rivers is texting me," she said to him, a frown of confusion on her face. He raised an eyebrow at her.

A: Oh. Hence the incorrect spelling of Bonjour

Unknown Number: Sorry

A: It's okay, rookie mistake.

A: Is this Alex?

Unknown Number: Who else calls you Freckles?

"Yes, this is definitely Alex Rivers, Carson," Avery looked at her friend. "She asked for my number a few days ago at Starbucks. I never thought she'd actually use it."

That was only partially the truth. Avery had expected Alex to message her on that same day asking for Carson's number. She figured that Alex must not have wanted to come on too strong by asking him for his number so instead she would ask her. But when Alex didn't message her that day, Avery presumed that the brunette must have had forgotten.

A: Do you want Carson's number?

Alex: LOL, no.

A: Oh

Alex: You look cute when you're confused

Avery felt her cheeks flush, and it wasn't due to the strong gush of chilly breeze that had just passed her.

"How do you know?" Carson asked Avery when she looked up from her phone. He leaned towards her, trying to get a peek but Avery had turned off the phone before he could read it. He raised both his eyebrows at his best friend's suspicious behaviour.

Avery chuckled uncomfortably, "Nevermind, it wasn't her. Just a wrong number."

****

There were many things Avery had always wanted when she was younger, but couldn't get. Whether it was for financial reasons, inconvenience or her mother simply saying 'no'. Out of all the things that she wanted, the thing she wished for most was a puppy. She had always begged and pleaded for one but her parents, specifically her mother, would never allow her to get one. But, a few days ago she had set up a presentation for her parents during Family Night about why she should get a dog and the reasons she brought up were compelling enough for them to give in. It was actually one reason in particular and that was that they could have the dog specially trained to detect the symptoms of her anxiety and help calm her down.

Her parents told her they would pick her up from school so that they could go pick up a puppy from the pet store. She was bursting with excitement.

Once the bell rang, signalling the end of the school day, she walked briskly towards her locker to take out her books. What she didn't expect to see was Alex leaning against her locker seeming to be waiting for someone. Avery wondered if she was waiting at the wrong locker.

Or maybe Avery got mixed up and the locker she was waiting at wasn't hers at all. But when she got close enough to see the number, she knew instantly that it was hers.

Reaching where Alex stood, Avery cleared her throat to guide Alex's attention from her phone to her.

"Um, hi Alex. Are you looking for someone?" Avery said awkwardly as she wrung her hands together. She was in a bit of a rush to get her puppy. She didn't even know if her parents were there yet but she had to be ready.

Alex could feel herself smiling inwardly at Avery's naivety. "Yes, actually. She's about this tall," Alex lifted her arm, palms facing down to indicate how tall the person was, "She has curly hair, brown eyes, caramel skin..." She paused, looking up at the ceiling. "Oh and freckles."

"Is it me?"

Alex scoffed, "Come on, Freckles. Don't be so self-absorbed."

"Oh." Avery felt her foot tapping as her impatience and eager increased. She really didn't have time for this. "Well, I'm sorry but I can't help you find her right now. Will you excuse me?"

Alex stepped to the side, giving Avery access to her locker.

"Are you in a rush? I wanted to talk to you," Alex frowned. "You never responded to my text today at lunch. I wanted to know if I overstepped my bounds." Ironically, Alex took a small step closer to Avery, giving her a chance to inhale her sweet coconutty smell with a hint of something else that she couldn't quite place her finger on.

"What do you mean?" Avery said, not looking at the girl for fear that she might get distracted. She switched out the books she didn't need tonight for the books that she did and then closed her locker.

"When I called you cute," Alex observed how the shorter girl stiffened before relaxing her shoulders. She smirked, "Which was the truth. I think you're adorable."

Avery felt her cheeks engulf in flames and she subconsciously brought her hands up to her face to cover them. "Thank you. I kind of have somewhere I need to be so... I'll talk to you later." Avery went to turn away.

She was starting to get the impression that Alex wasn't interested in Carson.

She began walking towards the exit of the building when she heard footsteps behind her. The tall girl didn't have to walk fast to catch up with Avery, within a second or two she was right beside her.

"Where are you going?"

"I'm picking up a puppy from the store with my parents."

"Exciting. Mind if I come with?"

Avery halted in her steps and looked at Alex confusedly. "Don't you have other, more 'bad girl' stuff to do?"

She was surprised to hear Alex let out a genuine laugh. "Is that what you think I am?" Alex asked with an amused smirk.

"Yeah, I mean... I don't know. That's just what I hear," Avery looked to the floor, "That you ride a motorcycle, you smoke drugs, drink alcohol and you're edgy and get into fights."

"I smoke drugs?" Alex asked teasingly. She shook her head, a small smile playing at her lips. Her smooth, very pink lips that made Avery question why she noticed them. "Aren't you in a hurry? Let's go."

The two went down the short flight of stairs at the entrance of the main building and towards the silver car that Avery spotted in the top right corner of the parking lot. Alex opened the door, allowing Avery to get in before she got in herself. Mr and Mrs Toussaint turned around, ready to greet their daughter and ask her about her day at school when they noticed that there was a stranger in their car. They exchanged glances.

"Maman, Papa, this is my friend Alex Rivers," Avery introduced, "Alex these are my parents, Elodie and Jean-Phillipe Toussaint."

The first thing Alex noticed was the stark difference in complexion between Avery's parents. She found Avery looked more like her father despite his blue eyes, but she could see where Avery got her mannerisms as the woman in front of her brought her eyebrows together with a frown.

"You can just call me Phillipe," Avery's father smiled warmly at the brunette, holding out his hand for her to shake. Alex was taken aback by his heavy accent, almost forgetting that the family was of French origin.

"You can call me Mrs Toussaint," Avery's mother smiled tightly, reaching out her hand as well after Alex had finished shaking her husband's.

Alex and Avery felt the car start once Mr Toussaint turned to face the steering wheel. Alex leaned closer to Avery making the shorter girl's breath hitch in her throat. "Your mom is a bit..." Alex whispered in Avery's ear before trailing off.

"She can be a bit protective. It takes a while for her to warm up to new people," Avery whispered back. Alex nodded in understanding.

Avery expected Alex to lean back to her former position in her seat, but the brunette just shifted slightly closer before sitting upright. Alex didn't expect it either, but she suspected it was because she felt something for the freckled girl. Interest? Fascination? Lust? She didn't know, all she knew was that she just wanted to be closer to her.

Ever since the sneezing incident and the party, Alex found herself out of her comfort zone when it came to Avery. She found herself craving Avery's attention, which was undoubtedly challenging to obtain. The girl was always in her own bubble and avoiding people unless they were named Carson Armani.

Silence settled between the four people in the car before Mrs Toussaint spoke up, "So Avery, where is Carson?"

Alex had a hunch that the mother was asking because she would have much rathered Carson tag along than someone else. She didn't blame the woman, Alex barely knew Avery much less her parents.

"He has football practice, maman."

"Football? You mean soccer," Alex raised an eyebrow as she looked over at Avery. "Last time I checked, Carson wasn't on the football team."

Avery groaned and rolled her eyes in annoyance.

Mrs Toussaint tilted her body and turned her head so that she could face Alex, "Avery hates when people call football 'soccer'. I take it that you two haven't been friends for that long."

Alex whispered into Avery's ear again, "You are nothing like your mother, personality-wise." Alex's whispering action sent a subconscious shivering sensation down Avery's spine as her breath tickled her ear.

"Yeah, I know I'm more like my father," Avery whispered back. 'Minus the anxiety,' she thought, but she didn't say that part.

Soon enough, the car slowed down as Mr Toussaint drove into a parking spot. The four of them exited the car and walked towards the large store in front of them. Avery was enticed by the many bright colours she could see on the inside and she perked up with excitement.

"I read that Golden Retrievers make really good therapy dogs," she stated to her mother as they stepped inside. Alex tilted her head to the side while the statement registered in her head. She ran her hand through her long hair uncomfortably, starting to get the feeling that this was probably a private family event. Avery didn't tell her not to come when she asked earlier, but then again Avery didn't say she could come either.

Alex walked towards the girl in question as she stared at some hamsters in a glass container. "Hey, are you comfortable with me being here? I never knew this was a family thing," Alex said sheepishly, rubbing the back of her neck. The sleeve of her shirt rolled up slightly with the motion, exposing a tattoo on her arm that attracted Avery's attention. Just as Avery started to decipher what it was, Alex put her arm down.

"Oh, it's okay we're just picking up a dog to help with my-" Avery paused before remembering that she and Alex have never really spoken about this before. Or about anything in particular really. She stood up properly, changing her position from bending over to look at the hamsters, and bit her lip. Despite that, she also remembered that Alex was there for her when she started to have an anxiety attack at the party a couple of weeks ago, so it should be okay to tell her.

"I mean you don't have to tell me, it's-"

Avery interrupted Alex to continue, "With my anxiety. I have General Anxiety Disorder, also known as G.A.D. It's more or less under control because I take Zoloft and I see a therapist twice a month, but sometimes it flares up and so it would be great to have a dog. I'm technically not looking for a therapy dog, just a dog that we can easily have trained to pick up on certain symptoms from time to time."

"Oh. Is that what was happening at the party when I took you to my room?"

"Yeah."

"Okay," Alex said, shoving her hands into her front pockets and rocking back on her heels. Avery felt extremely awkward and she felt her cheeks heat up.

"You blush a lot," Alex commented. "Let's go get your dog."

Alex walked off towards the canine section of the store, leaving Avery and her pink cheeks behind.

Chapter 8

- -

There was something special about reading that was like a drug to Avery. It was way more than just following a story. If that's what she wanted to do, she could just watch Netflix. But, reading books was something different. She didn't know if it was the intimacy felt between the reader and the characters, the smell and feel of the pages, the message or moral it conveys, the unique way different authors seem to make you feel like you're being dragged into the storyline or all of the above. Whether it was in French or English, Avery loved to read it.

This time it was a French novel that her mother had bought her named 'Pays Mêlé'. It was quite a solemn book and spoke about the struggles encountered by women and black people in the Caribbean 20th century.

Avery had reached the midway point of the book and decided to take a break there, her heart feeling too heavy to continue just yet. She placed her bookmark on the page where she stopped and closed the book, placing it beside her. She was sat on the steps of one of the side entrances to the school's main building since her teacher was absent. It was the first period of the day and everyone was in their classes, leaving the entire campus peaceful and quiet. The beautiful, well-trimmed grass was as green as ever and seemed to stretch on for miles now that there wasn't a crowd of students standing on it and blocking the view.

"Penny for your thoughts?" a voice sounded as Avery spotted a shadow in her peripheral. When she looked up, her eyes landed on Carson and she gave a small smile. Behind him though, Avery could decipher a figure if she squinted her eyes. Her smile seemed to falter.

"Who's that?" Avery asked, dismissing Carson's greeting. The person in question stepped out from behind her best friend and gave her a smile. She felt an unpleasant twinge in her stomach to see that Carson seemed to be hanging out with this random girl she didn't even know when he was supposed to be in class.

"Avery, this is Marigold," Carson used his hand to gesture to the red-head as he introduced her, "Marigold, this is my best friend Avery."

Marigold waved at Avery and held her hand out for a handshake. Her smile was almost blinding as Avery hesitantly met her halfway. "Hey!" said the random girl. Her voice sounded chirpy causing Avery to narrow her eyes in suspicion. Both her possessiveness and protectiveness for Carson kicked in and Avery analysed the girl from head to toe. There was no doubt that she was beautiful and Avery couldn't help but admire how the name 'Marigold' seemed to suit her so perfectly. Marigold's light hazel eyes almost seemed golden in the sunlight and the way it complemented her orange-red hair would make anyone think of the flower.

"Hello," Avery replied, letting go of her hand and turning her head to Carson, "What are you doing out here? It's not your free period yet."

"Marigold just transferred and Administration wanted me to show her around. So, that's what we're doing. What are you doing out here, Aves?"

Avery's eyes flicked back to the girl who she noticed was watching her just as carefully as she had been watching her before. "Seems a little inconvenient to be transferring in the middle of the semester during the last year of high school."

Carson furrowed his eyebrows at his best friend's icy tone.

Carson had only had one girlfriend during the period that he and Avery were friends. It's safe to say that it did not end well. She was a cheerleader and had only used his status for bragging rights and to ascend on the school's social ladder. Carson was a patient, passionate and kind person but he had to draw the line when said cheerleader started talking about their sex life. They parted ways, leaving Carson heartbroken.

He had dated more girls since then but they were brief as he kept finding out that they only wanted to be with him for similar reasons or to find out If he was as 'amazing in bed' as what his ex-girlfriend had said. Carson then decided to put dating on hiatus and so Avery couldn't be blamed for the way she reacted to Marigold.

Avery wasn't one to stereotype but Marigold's cheery attitude, somewhat tan skin, bright smile and toned calves led her to believe that she was another chienne of a cheerleader who would attempt to use her best friend. There was a price to being popular and well-liked and Avery would rather die than let Carson reap its consequences again. { bitch}

"Oh, I'm a junior," Marigold interjected.

Dying to get rid of the tense silence that settled among them, Carson spoke up. "Well, since you're new here why don't you sit with us at lunch."

Avery couldn't help but think that it was bold of Carson to assume that they'd be sitting together, especially now that she knew the redhead would be joining them. It was like Carson could read his friend's mind when he continued after a pause, "Right, Avery?"

Sometimes Avery felt that Carson was too nice for his own good. Not that she was mean, Avery was far from being a mean-spirited person. But, she wasn't too fond of people in general and kept to herself so that she wouldn't have to encounter situations like these. To her, that was one of the many perks of being a wallflower.

"Right, Carson," she sent her best friend a sickeningly sweet smile in response.

Carson leaned down to give his best friend a hug before saying quietly to her, "À bientôt et sois gentille, s'il te plait." With that, he and Marigold walked away to continue their tour, leaving Avery to her book once more. {See you soon and be nice, please}

****

Avery firmly believed that if she was a bit more rebellious, she would've just skipped school. Her mind was reeling from her Calculus and AP Physics classes and now that the bell had rung for lunch she had another thing to worry about. For a fleeting moment, her mind went to Alex and she was astonished at her thoughts when she found herself wondering what the tall girl would've done in a situation like this.

"Stab them." Think of the devil and she shall appear. Avery looked up at the girl with a confused look.

"You said 'what would Alex do?' out loud and I just happened to walk up to you at that moment," Alex clarified.
"I don't know what you're stressing about but stabbing
can be the solution to any problem. Forgot your homework? Stab the teacher. Got arrested for stabbing the
teacher? Stab the police officer."

Oddly, Alex's words brought a smile to Avery's face
as she exhaled a chuckle through her nose. The odd
pair talking to each other in the middle of the hallway
was starting to attract attention and Avery could feel the
eyes on her. Alex noticed when the freckled girl started
looking to the floor and her breath seemed to hitch and
she understood the situation.

"Well, good luck with whatever it is," Alex said nonchalantly, fixing her ponytail before walking off. She figured
it would save Avery's anxiety some trouble if people
saw that their encounter was brief so that they wouldn't
assume anything. The last thing Avery needed was to
have people poking fun at her again for sneezing on
Alex.

Avery took a deep breath in and walked outside. She
was exhausted and definitely not in the mood to play
nice with the Marigold girl. When she spotted her best
friend, he was sitting on a bench with the redhead sitting
across from him. They were chatting animatedly. The
sight caused Avery to scoff. Was Marigold too good to

sit on the grass like she and Carson normally did? She hoped Marigold would get her own new cheerleader friends and leave both her and Carson alone. Specifically Carson.

Avery took a seat next to Carson and took out her lunch. She had ravioli today, something she couldn't have eaten when she was on her diet which had ended ever since Carson persuaded her to have that pizza slice. She was excited for the chocolate chip cookies that she had packed and figured she would need the pick-me-upper for the next hour she was forced to face. In fact, who came up with the rule that dessert had to come before the plat principal. Yes, it was the French but since she was French she should be entitled to break that rule. {main dish}

Almost forgetting her manners, she mumbled a greeting to the two other people she was sat with before munching into her cookie. Carson replied by slinging his arm over her shoulder like he normally did, pulling her in for a side hug, and Marigold only sent her a small wave. Avery could tell from how much more silent Marigold got and the way she played with her food since Avery arrived, that she knew Avery was giving her the cold shoulder.

Feeling guilty, Avery joined the conversation, "So Marigold, what brings you to this fine establishment?"

She did her best attempt at a reassuring smile which made Marigold relax her shoulders as she smiled back.

"My parents and I were moving to this town, but I chose this school in particular because of the excellence of its soccer teams," Marigold spoke up, finally getting animated again.

At the mention of the word 'soccer', Carson's eyes lit up, "You play?"

Marigold scoffed playfully, "Do I?" Unzipping her bag, she flashed the two her shin guards, "I'm trying out for the girls' team this afternoon. I know all about you Carson 'Number Five' Armani and I hope I'll get to see you train one of these days."

Avery resisted the urge to roll her eyes. Just as she was trying to warm up to Marigold, she mentioned that she 'knew all about' Carson. For Avery, it was a complete red flag but at least she wasn't a cheerleader. Carson, on the other hand, just flicked his wrist like it was nothing, but Avery could see the slight shade of pink on his cheeks. She folded her arms.

"The girls' team trains on the field across from ours so we'd definitely see each other. In fact, the two teams even train together sometimes," Carson sent a smile to Marigold.

"That's so great! Where I'm from, the teams are totally separated because the boys don't want to train with us.

They treated our team like we were inferior to them. They were such pigs," Marigold huffed.

"Are you kidding me?" Carson furrowed his eyebrows in annoyance, "Girls are just as good as guys at soccer. Some of my favourite professionals are women. Marta, Rapinoe and Cristiane are my idols." Carson brought the tips of his fingers together on one hand and kissed them like an Italian chef.

"You just have to be a stereotype, don't you?" Avery teased her best friend.

"I'm an Armani. It's what we do," Carson joked back, imitating an Italian accent.

"Wow, you're Italian?" Marigold asked, her eyes sparkling with interest.

"Of Italian descent," Carson corrected. "I was born here."

"Have you ever been to Italy?"

"Yes, I have. I have aunts, uncles, cousins and my grandparents there."

Avery zoned out of the conversation, continuing to eat her lunch. She hoped Carson would turn Marigold down so that she wouldn't have to stick around for long or that maybe she could at least make her own friends. She was used to having to share him, but it wasn't usually when she was there with him. She knew she was getting his divided attention, but it felt like she was being ignored as the two chatted happily, not noticing how silent she was being.

A shout snapped her out of her thoughts and her head turned to the direction of the sound. Her eyes landed on a table to her far right and she saw where the shout had come from a blonde boy which she later made out to be Kaden Aldridge. Sitting at the table with him was Alex and two other people.

As if the brunette could feel someone's eyes on her, her gaze shifted from her friends and landed on Avery though they were some distance away. She smirked at the freckled girl, causing her heart to skip a beat as she looked away as quickly as possible, trying to bite down a smile.

Carson who had a smile on his lips and a bit of concern in his eyes, looked down at his best friend, "Hey Aves are you okay?" Avery nodded rapidly.

She was totally fine.

Chapter 9

"If you had three wishes, what would they be?" Avery asked as she laid on the grass. The breeze blew causing the blades underneath her to gently tickle her arm as she stretched it out to pet Milo. The small Golden Retriever yipped and started nip at the tips of her fingers.

"To never have to go to school again, to be able to fly and for America to lower its legal age for drinking," Alex responded. Time had flown and December was drawing near and most of the leaves on the trees had shed leaving a gorgeous sight on the ground for those who came to visit the park. "What would be yours?"

Avery sat up, her fingers playing with a single flower she found on a bush that seemed to take its time to shed its leaves. It was a week or two after Alex had accompanied Avery and the Toussaints to retrieve Milo and the girls found themselves spending a little more time with each other once Avery opened up. The two could comfortably say that they were friends rather than acquaintances. Today, Alex joined Avery while she walked Milo and they decided to take a break in the local park while they allowed the puppy to play.

"I'm not sure," Avery responded, "Maybe for world peace, the end of world hunger and for a bucket of chocolate chip cookies." Avery leaned over and placed the flower behind Alex's ear, causing the brunette to wrinkle her nose in distaste.

"Your answers make me sound like a shit person."

Avery let out a laugh, the sound causing Alex to look over at her. "Aren't you a bad person though?"

Alex smirked once she realised that Avery had censored her sentence, "Come on, say it, Avery."

"Say what?"

"Shit."

"No."

Alex raised herself up so that she was now resting back on her elbows. "Why don't you curse? Is it too dirty for you?" she teased.

"I do curse," Avery replied. Milo ran up to her with a stick in his mouth and jumped into her lap, earning a small smile from the freckled girl. She tossed it, expecting him to fetch the stick and bring it back only to observe that he stayed comfortably on her legs.

"I've never heard you curse before."

"I curse in French. Curse words in English don't sound nice. Plus we haven't really been talking for that long for you to judge whether or not I curse."

Alex scoffed, "Oh please. How long we've been talking has nothing to do with it. You hear me curse all the fucking time."

"Because your mouth is like a sailor's."

The corner of Alex's mouth turned upwards in a half smile, "Touché."

Milo jumped from Avery's lap, seemingly interested in Alex as he ran over to her and climbed on her chest to lick her face. Alex used a hand in an attempt to move the dog from her face but did not succeed. "This is like the worst kiss I've ever gotten," she groaned, moving her head from left to right trying to get the puppy to stop. "Way too much tongue, Milo."

"I have to drop him off for training tomorrow before school. Maman and Papa both can't do it this time," Avery said as she lifted Milo up from Alex's chest, holding him in the air and rubbing her nose against his. "I'm gonna miss you, little guy. Even if it's just for half a day," she spoke to him. Milo responded by licking Avery's nose.

"That's how people get worms," Alex commented as she got up from the grass. She brushed herself off before holding out a hand to Avery who graciously took it.

"I'd happily get worms from this little guy." Avery attached the leash to Milo's collar.

The girls continued along their walk with Milo teetering in front of them excitedly. Avery felt herself shiver as another gust of wind blew by. Winter was definitely approaching and Avery would need to wear warmer clothes. Alex's hand subconsciously went to the flower behind her ear, securing it as the day became windier.

"Tell me about your friends. What are they like? I know Carson's friends with Kaden, but that's about it," Avery winced when she mentioned Carson's name. She felt a pang of guilt when she thought about how she didn't inform Carson that she and Alex were friends now and when she lied to him about Alex texting her. But, they didn't have to tell each other everything right? Carson was her best friend and that would never change. It wasn't like Avery was blowing him off to spend time with Alex, she saw him just as often. That was when he wasn't training with Marigold.

"So there's Kaden who's a complete and utter goofball, kinda dumb, loves partying and is high like eighty per cent of the time. There's Sam. He's the 'sensible' one of all of us, I guess, and he's really smart. He's a dick but he's protective of the group, so maybe he's not all that dick-ish. And then there's Jason but we call him Long. He's the scary one that rarely talks and always plays with a switchblade."

"Why do you call him Long?" Avery asked, quite amused by her friend group. They sounded like interesting people.

"That's his last name, he's Asian."

Avery threw her hands up and let out a laugh, "Woah, you don't need to boast about your group's diversity to me just because I'm brown."

Alex punched Avery's shoulder lightly, "I'm not. If I was boasting I would have also stated that Sam is African American."

"You sound mighty proud. Nice to know you're not a racist," Avery joked. Her eyes spotted a familiar building and Alex watched as her eyes seemed to brighten. "Can we go for ice cream?"

"Sure, why not?" Alex shrugged. She looked on in amusement as Avery jogged across the street once she looked both ways. The freckled girl ran towards the ice cream store with Milo at her heels who must've thought that they were racing. Alex noticed that Avery could go from being awkward, nervous and anxious to excited and childlike in the blink of an eye. But there was something about Avery's laugh and smile that Alex found refreshing.

When Alex entered the store a few moments later, she found Avery standing in the middle of the store, Milo in one arm against her chest and a tester spoon of ice cream in the other hand. The sweet smell of ice cream invaded Alex's nose and the warm air from the heater inside relaxed her muscles.

"What are you getting?" Alex asked Avery when she finished tasting the ice cream she had sampled.

"I'm trying not to be predictable by getting cookies and cream so I think I'm going to go with strawberry cheesecake." Avery allowed Milo to lick the remnants from her small spoon as he had started to whine. "What are you getting?"

"Cookies and cream," Alex smirked at Avery who gasped.

"You can't do that!"

"Fine, I won't. I'll get..." Alex looked down at the flavours that were displayed, "Coffee."

Alex moved to talk to the girl at the counter who was waiting for them to make their order, "Hey, could I get coffee and strawberry cheesecake. Two waffle cones."

"Coming right up. You and your girlfriend make a cute couple, by the way."

Alex, not expecting the young girl's comment, cleared her throat and rubbed the back of her neck. Avery observed the brunette, noticing her actions while bouncing Milo against her chest like a baby. She had learned that Alex only did that when she felt awkward, just like when they were at the pet store.

"We're not together," Alex said. She didn't understand why the comment threw her off like that. She was normally cool and composed, but now it felt like her body and brain didn't know how to react. She cleared her throat once more and ran a hand through her hair.

"Oh?" the girl's eyes brightened, "Then you wouldn't mind giving me your number?"

"Oh, sorry, I have a girlfriend. It's just not...her," Alex's eyes flicked away from the girl's face. Why did she lie? Why didn't she want the cute employee's number? Frustration jabbed at her and Alex huffed, "Look, can I just get the ice creams? This is what this place is for, right? Selling ice cream and not imposing on people's private lives?"

Avery frowned in concern once she heard Alex's voice rise and she stopped rocking Milo in her arms, letting him down onto the floor. Alex's voice wasn't loud enough for her to hear the conversation, but it was loud enough for her to know that she was upset.

When Alex walked back to Avery, she had two cones of ice cream in either hand and an annoyed expression on her face. Avery followed behind the taller girl as she led them to a booth in the far corner of the store and they sat down across from each other. Alex handed Avery her cone once she had placed Milo on the seat next to her and her hands were free.

"Thank you. You didn't have to pay, you know?" Avery said graciously. Alex only shrugged, beginning to lick her ice cream, ignoring Milo's yips for her to share.

"It's so nice that they allow dogs here," Avery commented after a moment of silence. This time, Alex only hummed in agreement.

Avery sighed and looked down on the table before using her tester spoon from before to scoop a bit of her ice cream and give it to Milo. He wagged his tail in delight and his tongue licked up the dairy treat. She was so happy that she now had a puppy and that they seemed to get along splendidly. Milo had school four days a week for the next month or so in order to get him trained. It was nice to know that while she was off at school, so was he, and in the evenings they would be reunited again for him to sleep in his new doggy bed that was placed at the foot of hers.

"Are you okay? What happened up there?" Avery decided to ask. She knew that Alex was upset and so the silence felt tense; it made her anxious knowing that something wasn't right and she didn't know what it was.

"She asked for my number," Alex responded nonchalantly, deciding to omit the part where the girl called them a cute couple.

"Oh," Avery's voice was quiet as she twiddled her thumbs underneath the table, "But don't you like girls? I mean- I don't mean to assume, but it's just what I hear... at school. "

Alex looked up from her ice cream cone at Avery. The way her messy bun was perched on her head and how the small curls that were too short to reach it framed her face. The way her eyebrows seemed to come together as she looked down at the table and her lower lip jutted out only slightly as she frowned. Alex looked down at her ice cream cone again, trying not to look at the girl in front of her and she sighed, "Yes, I do. But, it's not that. I just-"

Alex didn't know how to explain it since she barely understood it herself.

"I get it. You have people throwing themselves at you at school all the time. Like, you're so popular. You just wanted to get away from it for a while, so maybe her coming on to you made you a bit upset," Avery tried to meet her halfway there once she noticed that Alex didn't know how to finish her sentence.

Alex thought that maybe Avery was right. Maybe that was the reason, she was just exhausted by all these people.

"Anyway, I never thought I'd see the day when there would be another expression on Alex Rivers' face that wasn't a smirk," Avery tried to poke fun at her friend, sending down more ice cream on a spoon for Milo once he started yipping again.

In response to her tease, Alex smirked, "Don't tell me you missed it, Freckles."

Avery didn't want to admit that she kind of did.

Chapter 10

A very and Carson sat curled up by her reading nook, each holding a mug of hot chocolate. It was now early December and the first snow was due to fall. The temperature outside had gotten really cold at what seemed to be lightning speed. Avery was deep in thought as she looked out the window. The beautiful multi-coloured leaves were now gone leaving patches of almost grey looking grass and stark naked tree branches. The period before the snow was always the ugliest. When the sky was grey, everything looked apocalyptic and Avery half-expected to see a horde of zombies on the h o r i - zon.

Avery was snapped out of her head when Carson picked up the can of whipped cream from the floor. "Refill?" he offered. She nodded her head and reached out her mug to him, her whipped cream from before already melted.

Carson topped her up before himself, making spirals with the fluffy substance until it reached the brim of her cup.

"I-," they both started at the same time. Carson chuckled and shook his head while Avery gave a sheepish smile.

"I have something I want to tell you, " Carson spoke up after they spent a moment staring at each other, both waiting for the other to start.

"Me too," Avery chimed in. "But, you go first."

Carson adjusted himself under the throw that covered both their legs. They were facing each other, one on either side of the reading nook and their knees were touching. The nook was only made for one person and Carson was tall, but the extra body heat was greatly appreciated.

"I think I like Marigold," Carson blurted out to his best friend. His cheeks and the tips of his ears were pink and Avery knew it wasn't just from the temperature. "I know you don't trust her and I don't expect you to trust her that easily, given my history with girls. But, I just wanted to let you know. She seems like a really genuine and amazing girl and I think she likes me too."

Avery frowned. It was no secret that she was still unsure of how she felt about Marigold, even the redhead
herself knew. At first, she had taken offence but once
Carson explained why she became more understanding.

Carson looked down at his hot chocolate, anxiously
waiting for his best friend to say something. Her opinion
meant the world to him and Avery knew that. Avery
couldn't find anything wrong with Marigold and oh did
she try. But as Carson said, she seemed really genuine
and down to Earth. If it wasn't for her protectiveness,
Avery figured she and Marigold would have been able
to get on by then.

Avery couldn't deny the chemistry between the two
when she saw them together. Plus, they had so much
in common and Marigold didn't seem to be interested
in popularity. Avery could honestly say that she didn't
seem like that type of girl.

"Okay," Avery smiled at Carson, causing his head to
rise back up as he looked at her with wide eyes. Looking
at the expression on his face, she was reminded that she
would never want to get in the way of his happiness.

His face broke into a grin, "Really?" Avery nodded.

"She's a nice girl and you two have chemistry. Plus,
you'd make a super cute couple. I just want to see you

happy, Carson. And love, well, it's a risk," Avery said honestly, reaching her free hand over to hold his.

"Thank you. What was it that you wanted to say?"

Carson's question made her remember what she wanted to tell him and anxiety settled in her chest and stomach. It felt like her chest had caved in and her throat had closed up. Avery gripped Carson's hand, trying to calm herself down.

Seeing the distress in his friend's eyes, he rubbed circles into the back of her hand with his thumb in an attempt to calm her down. Avery took a look around the room, registering where she was, identifying mint-green objects and trying to breathe slowly. She ignored the nauseous feeling at the pit of her belly and tried to clear her mind of the negative and worrisome thoughts that had previously flooded.

Taking one last deep breath, she spoke. "I think... I think I like girls."

She tried her best to look Carson straight in the eyes and not look down at her lap. She felt her eyes start to water as the nanoseconds that flew by waiting for his reaction felt like minutes; hours even.

"Oh, Aves," he breathed. He put their mugs down on the windowsill and stretched over to give his best friend a bear hug.

"I love you so much, okay?" he whispered into her ear. Avery nodded into his shoulder, her breath coming out shakily as she started to cry. It was like a huge load lifted off of her chest now that she had told her best friend. Once she found out, she knew she had to tell him.

"I love you too."

The two let each other go and Carson went to ruffle Avery's hair but this time she let him.

"When did you know?"

Avery chuckled through her tears and sniffed, "Yester-day. Are you surprised?"

Carson shook his head with a smile, "I've had a feeling. I've caught you checking out girls before, but I don't even think you knew you were. At first, I thought it was because you're an observant person that likes to watch the world go by. But that changed when I realised that you would stare at the girls way longer than the guys."

Avery blushed, "Well that's just because girls are more aesthetically pleasing than guys."

"And that's why you're a lesbian," Carson said, making the both of them laugh. "Are you going to tell your parents?"

"One step at a time," Avery paused, glancing out the window, "Oh, it's snowing."

****

Avery stood in the doorway of her house's main entrance, seeing Carson off as he left. A few moments after he had driven off and she closed the door to preserve the heat inside, Avery felt her phone vibrate.

Alex: I'm bored. WYA?

A: At my house. Where else?

Alex: Oh right

Alex: Forgot you don't have a life.

Avery rolled her eyes, a small smile playing at her lips and she inserted a shrugging emoji.

Alex: Come over

A: In case you haven't noticed, it's snowing outside.

Alex: Barely

Alex: You don't like snow?

A: Oh, I love snow.

Alex: Alright well come over

A: That's enough logic for me *eye roll emoji*

Alex: Okay so see you in 10

Avery scoffed at the girl's response to her sarcasm. She jogged all the way up her stairwell and went inside her room to put on some warmer clothes. She had only been to Kaden and Alex's mansion-like house once before and hoped she remembered the directions.

But it turned out, she didn't have to. As Avery was combing her hair in front of the mirror on her vanity, her phone buzzed once more with a message from Alex giving her the location of her house. Neither of her parents was home so she sent them both a message letting them know that she was leaving the house before forwarding them the address. She grabbed her purse, started her car and soon she was off.

When she arrived at the Aldridges' house, she couldn't help but let out a tiny gasp. The house was even more beautiful during the daylight than it was at night. Granted, the grass on the lawn was a brownish-grey and the bushes and trees were bare, but it was a step up from when she had last seen it. Hundreds of red cups and drunk teenagers littered across the lawn didn't do the estate much justice.

Avery parked her car and ascended the slight slope of steps. She rang the doorbell before stuffing her hands into the pockets of her coat, rocking back and forth on her heels as she waited. When the door finally swung open, Avery's eyes settled on the tall brunette that stood in front of her. She was wearing sweatpants that were rolled up to her knees and a tank top, yet she could be mistaken for a goddess. It was the first time Avery had seen Alex with her hair down and she admired its length as it rested by her waist. She wished she could run her fingers through it, just to see how it felt.

Alex was now smirking at the shorter girl, leaning against the doorway as she waited for her to come in.

"You're letting in all the cold air, you know?" she said, bringing Avery's mind back from wherever it went. She smiled sheepishly and stepped inside.

Now that it wasn't crowded, the house seemed much larger than it did on the night of the party. Avery tried not to stare but found herself doing so as her eyes explored the entrance room and the stairwell leading to the next two floors, finally landing on the chandelier above them.

"Oh. So you're rich rich," Avery commented resulting in a chuckle from Alex.

"No, Kaden's dad is," she said as she gestured with her hand for Avery to follow after she had taken off her boots. Avery walked behind Alex quietly as she led them up the stairs and to the second floor. She felt a bit awkward and out of place, which was evident in the way she wrung her hands together.

The two stopped in front of a door which Avery assumed was Alex's. Her suspicions were confirmed when the girl opened the door and Avery was met with the same lifeless room she was in once before. Shrugging off her coat, Alex took it from her and folded it, placing it on a stool that was nearby.

Alex observed the slight frown that rested on Avery's face as the shorter girl looked around. Avery had hoped that since she had been there, Alex had put up at least a few decorations or something. "You alright, Freckles?"

Not wanting to offend Alex in any way, Avery nodded, deciding not to voice her opinion. Alex only shrugged and went to sit in her loveseat.

"I thought you were bored- No, don't do that!" exclaimed Avery. Alex paused, hair tie held by her lips as both her hands were in her hair; previously in the process of twisting it into a bun.

"I-um. I mean... it looks nice when it's down," Avery mumbled, her cheeks heating as she went to sit on the bed. She looked to the side in an attempt to avoid the curious girl's gaze. Alex slowly lowered her hands and removed the hair tie from her mouth.

"You're a strange girl, Avery Toussaint," Alex commented.

"Toussaint."

"Toussaint."

"Toussaint," this time Avery said it slower.

"Toussaint."

"Oui, Toussaint," Avery said with a smile. Alex was getting closer.

"Croissant."

Avery grabbed a pillow from the bed and threw it at Alex, laughing in the process. Alex rolled her eyes, giving a small chuckle as well.

"You gonna tell me what's up, Freckles? I don't bite."

"You sure look like you do."

Alex only smiled, biting her tongue as she sat back in her seat. She kept looking at the freckled girl, waiting for her to talk. Avery didn't know if it was the tense silence or Alex's gaze, but she opened her mouth after a few moments.

"I don't want to be that person and I know it's not a big deal, but your room feels so... not you. I don't know if that makes sense," Avery looked to her lap.

"That's because this isn't my room," Alex said nonchalantly, her eyes still on Avery. "Well, it's my room but not my room."

Avery looked back up at Alex with a confused stare. What did that even mean? As if in response to her thoughts, Alex stood up and walked to a door that was located not so far from her loveseat.

"Come on," Alex said softly as she twisted the doorknob.

Chapter 11

"Come on," Alex said softly, twisting the doorknob. She stepped in before Avery, prompting the shorter girl to follow her inside. The sight that she laid her eyes on evoked a small gasp from her. For some reason, Alex had another room inside her room and the thought made Avery's head hurt.

"I've never brought anyone in here, to be honest," Alex said sheepishly, rubbing the back of her neck.

Avery very much preferred this room to the one she was in before. The walls were painted forest green and seemed to be filled with more interesting objects and decorations. There was a black, grand piano in the corner of the room and perched against the wall next to it was a guitar case. As she slowly walked around the room, observing her surroundings, she let her fingers run over the lid of the piano; she never would have pegged Alex as a musician.

The wall opposite to her was lined with a few stickers of black music notes blending in so perfectly that it looked like they were painted on. There were Polaroid pictures hung up on a single string of lights that hung from the ceiling on that same wall; they held the images of cities around the world, from Paris to Budapest.

"It's gorgeous in here," Avery breathed. There was a smaller bed in the room and above it hung a couple of posters of legendary musicians including Stevie Wonder and Frank Sinatra. The bed looked extremely comfortable with its fluffed up black comforter and bounteous white pillows. There was a simple, matte black bookshelf that sat next to it which held many books that caught Avery's attention.

She walked over to the bookshelf and sat on the edge of the bed, Alex following her actions. Avery plucked a classic book from the row, 'To Kill A Mockingbird' by Harper Lee, and flipped through the crisp pages.

"Satisfied?" Alex asked, a little nervous.

"Very," Avery responded with a smile as she looked down at the book in her hands.

"I'm glad." Alex let out a breath she didn't even know she was holding. The opposite happened for Avery though, as Alex gently took her hand out of the blue.

The brunette stood up from the bed, causing Avery to do the same after returning the book to its position on the bookshelf.

Alex led her to the stunning piano and the two sat on the piano bench. A small paper that was on the wall next to the large instrument caught Avery's attention. It was a certificate for a competition that Alex had won and Avery smiled at how it was hung proudly, now knowing that music was something very important to Alex.

"Alexia Rivers?" Avery asked, reading the name that was printed in bold letters.

Alex scoffed and reached over to turn the certificate over. "Alex Rivers," she corrected the freckled girl.

Avery shook her head. "Alexia," she tried it out, "I like it."

The sound of Alex's full name on Avery's tongue brought a small blush to the brunette's cheeks. She chose not to comment and instead placed her hands on the keys of the piano. Avery observed as the taller girl took a deep breath in and started to play. She noticed how Alex's lips parted slightly in concentration as her fingers gently stroked the keys, creating a beautiful melody. Avery closed her eyes, taking in the music, only to open them again in surprise when a smooth voice started to sing.

Cold bones

Yeah, that's my love

She hides away, like a ghost

Oh, does she know that we bleed the same?

Oh, don't wanna cry but I break that way

She closed her eyes once more, taking in the beauty of the music accompanied by Alex's astonishingly beautiful voice. It was refreshing to finally be exposed to Alex's vulnerability and begin to learn about who she was. They had been speaking for weeks now and yet, Avery had never been exposed to this side of the fascinating girl that sat beside her.

As her brain digested the lyrics of the song, she rested her head on Alex's shoulder.

I got a fear

Oh, in my blood

She was carried up into the clouds

High above

Oh, if you're bled, I'll bleed the same

Oh, if you're scared, I'm on my way

Did you run away? Did you run away? I don't need to know

If you ran away, if you ran away,

Come back home

Just come home.

Avery was almost disappointed by the discontinuation of the soothing voice that lulled her into such a calm state.

"Are you asleep?" Alex asked with a hint of humour in her tone. Avery shook her head in response, her eyes still closed and her position unchanged.

"Another one," she requested quietly. Alex nodded and placed her fingers on the piano once more.

****

"I never knew you were a reader," Avery commented as she continued going through Alex's collection of books on her bookshelf.

"As you can see, there are a lot of things you don't know about me, Freckles," Alex smirked, spread out on the soft bed, observing the curly-haired girl as she flipped through the pages of every book.

Avery paused and closed the book she was holding. She was sprawled out on the floor next to the low bookshelf to better obtain the books she wanted to look at. She placed the book in her lap and looked up at Alex, her cheeks heating after realizing that the brunette was already looking at her.

"Why?" she asked. Alex raised an eyebrow in question.

"You said I'm the first person that's been in here. Why? Why do you even have another room inside your room in the first place?" Avery clarified.

"I'm a reserved person and I don't need people in my business," Alex shrugged before she flipped over on the bed to lay on her back.

"But what about your friends?"

Alex let out a chuckle, "We don't talk about interests and feelings or other stuff like that. We just like to have fun."

The freckled girl nodded in understanding, not that she could relate. She realised 'interests and feelings' were something she and Carson often spoke about as she recounted the events from that morning.

"Besides, you're my friend too," Alex added, making Avery smile softly to herself.

"Mine too, Alexia."

"Alex."

"Alexia."

"Alex."

"Alexia."

"Croissant."

Avery seriously contemplated throwing the book she was holding in her hand. But, she couldn't bring herself to do that to the poor book... and Alex. She looked at the cover page once more, 'The Rest of Us Just Live Here' by Patrick Ness.

"Could I borrow this?" she asked Alex with pleading eyes. Alex's gaze shifted to the blue book that Avery held in her hands.

"I haven't read it yet," Alex started but was cut short when Avery's facial features contorted to the puppy face she often used to get cookies from her mother. There was something about how the freckled girl's eyebrows drew together, her already large eyes growing even bigger and her pink lower lip jutting out that swayed Alex to mutter a small 'okay'.

She took notice to the grin that was now blossoming on Avery's face and she rolled her eyes, willing herself to look away. The way Avery made her feel was abnormal and it made her slightly uncomfortable. There was a slight possibility that Alex could have feelings for her, but she didn't want to think about that at the moment. Besides, she could just be misinterpreting a soft spot for a crush.

"Well, it's been a couple of hours and the guys are coming over soon. So unless you want an early introduction," the brunette trailed off, giving Avery the option to leave.

Avery bit her bottom lip in consideration. She wasn't a people person and she wasn't sure she was ready to meet all of Alex's friends yet, but she found her mouth opening and the following words spilling out,

"They sounded like pretty cool people the last time we spoke about them. So, sure."

Alex's eyebrows shot up in surprise at the shorter girl's statement. Her look of astonishment was soon replaced with a small smile as she got up from the bed. Avery followed in her actions, brushing the back of her jeans as she stood up from the floor by reflex. When she first realised the tidiness of the room, there was no doubt in her mind that the Aldridge-Rivers had housekeepers who kept the place as pristine as it appeared. It was only after that she remembered what Alex had said about no one coming in here but herself.

In the time they had spent together in Alex's secret room, Avery had come to learn way more about the brunette than she did previously. She learned that Alex was a lover of music, a reader, organised, tidy and reserved. She was drawn to darker colours but was not afraid of variety. From the room and the outfits that Avery had seen her wear, it would be difficult not to notice that Alex's favourite colour seemed to be a forest or dark green. She also learned that Alex was a damn good pianist and singer.

She couldn't wait to see Alex when she was surrounded by her friends. Would her green eyes brighten in amusement? Would her smile captivate the entire room? Avery was desperate to hear a hearty laugh from the taller girl, one that wasn't soft or a throaty chuckle. One that would make her heart soar and sound like music to her ears.

Getting to know Alexia Celeste Rivers was turning out to be better than any book she had read, any autumn she anticipated or any chocolate chip cookie she consumed.

Chapter 12

The pair exited the room and Avery observed as Alex locked the door with a small, golden key. The brunette glanced at the freckled girl and she looked away, giving Alex privacy to stash the key wherever she kept it. She didn't expect, though, for the girl in question to place her fingers under her chin, bringing Avery to look at her.

"I trust you," Alex said simply, before stepping backwards. Soon her touch was gone as quick as it came, but the sensation was left lingering on Avery's skin. Alex carefully placed the key inside a small grey chest and pushed it under the large chest of drawers that stood next to the right corner of the room.

A loud noise followed by boisterous shouts made Avery visibly jump in her spot. She put her hand on her chest and exhaled deeply in an attempt to slow her quickening heart rate.

"Relax, it's just the boys. I need to remind them not to slam the doors," Alex crossed her arms. "You'd think Kaden would care more since it's his house."

Avery let out a nervous chuckle.

Why did she agree to this again?

The brunette exited the room, prompting Avery to follow in her footsteps. She found herself doing that a lot lately. The trip down the stairs to the common room felt short as she started to dread the formal introduction that was yet to come. 'Formal' in the sense that when she met the boys, it was at the party almost two months ago and she barely even caught their names before Carson was whisked away from her.

She tried to distract herself from the anxiety welling in her chest by admiring the way Alex's silky and volu-minous, dark hair bounced about her waist with every confident stride she took. The sweatpants she wore accentuated her hips and their movement and the ob-servation brought a blush to Avery's cheeks. Maybe her thoughts went a bit too far there.

As they approached the common room, Alex ran her hand through her hair before swiftly catching it into a ponytail as if she could sense Avery's eyes on it. The freckled girl knew that that wasn't the case, but she couldn't help but wonder why she was putting her hair up now that her guy friends were here. When they were upstairs, after Avery's request for her to leave it down, she seemed so comfortable with her hair spilling over her shoulders and down her back.

Too caught up in her thoughts, Avery hadn't realised that Alex had stopped in her path at one of the many entrances to the room, causing the freckled girl to walk into her back. If Alex was bothered she didn't show it as she cleared her throat to gain the attention of Kaden and Sam who were bickering over something minuscule and Jason whose eyes were trained on his pocket knife.

"How many times do I have to remind you about slamming the fucking doors?" Alex narrowed her eyes, her hands now on her hips. If it were any other person, Avery would find herself giggling at the stance and tone of voice as she had only ever seen her mother scold that way. But with Alex, it was intimidating and with the silence that travelled around the room, Avery could sense that she wasn't the only one affected.

"Hey sis," Kaden broke the silence with a large grin.

"I told you not to call me that," Alex responded, rolling her eyes at her step-brother.

"Who's that behind you?" Sam asked, pointing towards the shorter, more freckled girl who at that point wished she could blend in with the surroundings.

"Oh," Alex stepped to the side, ridding Avery of a hiding place, "Guys, this is Avery. Avery, that's Sam

Earwood, Jason Long and you already know Kaden Aldridge."

"Is that Freckles?" Kaden wiggled his eyebrows at Alex in a teasing manner.

"Shut up."

"Hi," Avery waved sheepishly, her voice coming out in a squeak. Her eyes bulged when she saw the knife in Jason's hands, but the smiles on Jason's, Alex's and Kaden's faces brought a soft smile to her own.

"Cute," Jason smirked, before looking down at his blade once more. Avery brought her eyebrows together in confusion. Wasn't he supposed to be the scary one that doesn't talk?

"Take a seat, Freckles," Alex gently pulled Avery's hand as she walked towards a sofa then she sat down, patting the seat next to her. Avery obliged, with a slight blush.

****

Avery couldn't understand how the school had dubbed Alex and her friends as the 'bad kids'. Sure they did some risky and illegal things from time to time but they were sat in the living room playing Mario Kart and Avery believed that no bad person would ever play Mario Kart. Avery could see why others would be intimidated by Jason and Alex. Sam, from the way he sent her glares every five minutes, could be perceived as cold or mean. But, Kaden was just a ball of fluff.

His go-to Mario Kart character? Princess Peach.

In normal circumstances, Avery would feel uncomfortable and out of place from the looks Sam kept giving her and maybe it was the fact that she shared a sofa with Alex and the way their arms brushed together each time they moved, but she couldn't care less. Now, Avery had never had a crush before, but if she had, she imagined it would feel just like the way it did when she and Alex made physical or eye contact.

"So, Freckles," Sam added an emphasis to Avery's nickname which rubbed her the wrong way, "Does Number Five know you're here?"

She let her eyes leave the screen briefly to glance at the boy's cocky smirk. He knew that he had struck a nerve by the way she tensed up. Villager's motorcycle fell off the track on Avery's section of the screen.

"No, but I'm sure he wouldn't mind. I saw him this morning," Avery tried to speak up confidently, smiling softly.

"Why not invite him to the party then?"

Avery's heart jumped in her chest. If she were to call Carson, he would ask what she was doing at Kaden/Alex's house. Then, she'd have to explain that she was invited over and there was no way it would just happen randomly. So she'd have to tell him that she and Alex had been friends for the past month or so and she just never told him. The two had never lied or omitted information from each other before. It would be the start of the end of their friendship and Avery couldn't bear to lose her best friend.

"He has football practice and this game only allows four players. You're already sitting out, it wouldn't be fun if another person had to too," Avery's voice gradually became shaky.

"Soccer? It's snowing outside, Freckles-"

"Can you please not call me that," Avery's voice was strained as her hands tightened around the remote.

"-Plus we can always switch to a different game," Sam continued, ignoring Avery's plea.

"Samuel," Alex warned in a low tone.

"Why don't you want to call your best friend, Freckles?" Sam pressed.

Avery could feel the clenching of her chest and the previous atmosphere of the evening had shattered as she started to hyperventilate. She pressed the 'plus' icon on her console to pause the game and sat back in the sofa.

"Does he even know you're friends with Alex?"

Kaden's face was set in one of confusion as he looked between his friend and the small girl now hugging herself on the couch and Jason sat with a deep frown on his face. Neither knew or understood what was going on at the moment. Sam could be judgemental or insensitive at times, but they had never seen this side of him before.

Avery felt as if her blood was running cold. If Carson left, she'd have no one. Carson was a part of her now, a part of her family. She didn't deserve him. She knew she didn't. He was always her better half. Everyone loved Carson, nobody knew Avery. People had always wondered why such a popular guy would be friends with such a nobody, but Avery and Carson had never questioned it. They were just them.

She was afraid that if Carson found out she had been lying to him, it would break him. She had always been protective of him and his heart; she gave Marigold hell because she believed that the redhead would break his heart but now it was herself who would be doing the deed. She would break him and this time it would be Marigold putting back the pieces. But who would keep Avery together?

"Are you ashamed of us? Ashamed of Alex?" Sam continued.

Avery couldn't feel the tears running down her face, couldn't feel the protective arm Alex had thrown around her, couldn't hear Sam's last comment. All she could feel was emptiness surrounding her, it was like it had swallowed her. She wanted to escape the skin that enveloped her. She felt like she was dying.

"Avery?" Alex dropped to the floor in front of the girl, holding her face with both her hands in an attempt to get her to look her in the eyes. Instead, it was like the freckled girl looked right through her.

"Why the fuck would you do that, Sam?!" she shouted back at her friend. Her heart broke as she kept her eyes trained on Avery who was now trembling in her arms. She needed to calm her down. She needed to help her breathe, but she didn't know how to.

"Shit, shit, shit, shit, shit," Alex repeated as she rubbed circles on Avery's cheeks with her thumbs, occasionally wiping her tears away. "Kaden, call Carson."

At the sound of her best friend's name, Avery broke down into hysterics. Throughout everything, Carson had always trusted her and she had never done anything to break that. She didn't know what it was about Alex. She didn't know if it was that she thought Carson would disapprove or if she just didn't want to share what she had with Alex. She didn't even fully know if she had anything with Alex to share in the first place.

But Avery wasn't stupid. She had a sense of how Alex felt for her. She caught the few times that Alex had flirted with her, calling her cute. She noticed how Alex had kept the flower in the hair after Avery had placed it there, how agitated she was at the ice cream store when the employee asked her for her number, how Avery was the first person to ever see Alex's secret room. She wasn't sure of Alex's feelings, but she had a clue. But then again, her own feelings could be clouding her judgement. Then she would've kept a secret for nothing.

Avery couldn't breathe anymore. The small amount of oxygen going to her lungs due to the hyperventilation had now decreased to none. It was like her throat closed up and she was suffocating. Her vision was going and she attempted to look into Alex's eyes now that she was holding her up, but she couldn't. She couldn't focus, she couldn't think, she couldn't breathe. Her chest was racked with her sobs as she grew more hysterical. She wanted to scream, but nothing could come out.

"We're losing her! Goddammit, Kaden, just fucking call Carson," Alex was shouting now. In a desperate attempt to help the freckled girl regain consciousness, the brunette placed a chaste kiss to her damp forehead.

"Come on, Avery. Please stay with me? I don't know what to do and I can't get out of this situation by stabbing you," she joked.

"I called Armani," Kaden rushed up to Alex, his smartphone tightly clutched in his hand. "Also, I'd advise you not to look back."

Alex's head snapped to the side and she tilted her body to better see what Kaden was referring to.

"Are you kidding?" Kaden muttered at his stepsister, before standing up and heading to the kitchen. "I'll go get some ice for Freckles."

"We seriously don't need this right now," Alex sighed at the sight before her. Sam was on the floor and Jason was on top of him, beating him to a pulp.

Chapter 13

Alex carefully observed the features on the face of Avery's best friend. Tiny beads of sweat dotted his forehead and his blond hair was messy from the many times he ran his hand through it. They had just driven Avery to her house and placed her on her bed so that when she woke up she'd be in a familiar environment. Alex let her eyes stray to the unconscious girl, her golden retriever puppy curled up on her chest. Milo lifted his head every few minutes to lick the face of his owner.

Alex couldn't help but admire how beautiful and peaceful Avery looked even though she was unconscious.

"How did you say she ended up at your house again?" Carson asked with a sigh of frustration. But the brunette could see the worry etched in his eyes.

"I invited her over so she could help me with my French. The session ran a little late and the boys came over. Sam said some dick-ish things and she had a panic attack- you know how he has no filter," the lie ran off her tongue smoothly.

Carson nodded, wiping his forehead with the back of his hand. "Oh yeah, I remember her saying that you asked her for her number about a month ago. It makes sense it was for tutoring. What was Sam saying?"

Alex glanced at the girl that laid on the bed. Guilt racked her chest for the words she was about to say, but she kept her facial features nonchalant to give the illusion that she didn't care as much as she actually did. "He mentioned how you're popular, I guess, and she's not. And he asked why you guys were friends."

Alex absolutely despised what she said and she loathed herself for saying it, but she knew Carson didn't know she and Avery were friends and she knew how Avery felt about telling him. At that point, it wasn't about keeping their friendship a secret anymore, it was about the fact that Avery had lied to him.

Carson's hands balled themselves into fists as his blood boiled. "Where is he?" he almost growled between gritted teeth.

"Don't worry, Jason already has that covered. Sam was sent to the E.R. He may be quiet and violent but Long has a soft spot for those who appear vulnerable." Alex had never seen Carson angry before. He was known for being everyone's favourite person; kind, sweet, funny and charming. But she understood the rage that he must have been feeling at that point because she felt it too.

Carson let out one more sigh and Alex watched his facial features relax. He leaned over to Avery's sleeping body to ruffle the fur of the dog that lay on her chest. "I'm going to go talk to her parents. Please keep an eye on her, call us if she wakes up," Carson said, retracting his hand and placing it in his front pocket. Alex only nodded at him before he turned around and exited the room.

She glanced around the room, taking in the light greens and whites that coloured the room. This was exactly the type of room she could picture for Avery. There were some framed quotes in French that she didn't know the translation to and could only admire the font. The room looked like Avery, smelt like Avery, felt like Avery and it put a small smile on Alex's face.

Alex let her eyes scan the pictures that were hung around the room. Most were family pictures or pictures with Carson. Someone wouldn't have to be a genius to tell that he was a big part of Avery's life.

Alex slowly walked around the room until a particular picture caught her attention. It was a picture of Avery when she was about 3 years old. Her curly hair was a bit wavier back then and was brought into a small top-knot on her head. Avery's eyes sparkled with mischievousness as she leaned forward on her high chair towards the plate of cookies on the dinner table. The picture must have been taken before their move as Alex could spot a French flag at the corner of the picture. Avery's now bronze skin was much lighter, making her look almost Caucasian. Alex could only imagine the drama that could have ensued if it was her father that was black and her mother that was white.

Once she had finished exploring Avery's room, Alex sat at the edge of the bed took out her phone. She had a couple missed calls from Kaden and a few messages.

Kaden: How is she?

Kaden: How are you?

Kaden: Is everything okay?

She sighed and called him. The line rang for a couple of times before she was able to hear his voice on the other side.

"Hey Lex," his voice was exasperated. "What's going on?"

Alex glanced towards the freckled girl not so far from her before responding. "Not much. We have her at her house and we're waiting for her to wake up. Carson went to talk to her parents. They're not really happy right now, which is expected."

"Long is still pretty pissed. I think. He was pretty silent and he was just staring at everyone here. I sent him home, just in case. Sam is just frowning on the hospital bcd they gave him. He refuses to talk about what happened so we're kinda just waiting until the doctor gives him the 'okay' to leave."

Alex's grip on her phone tightened and her voice became tight, "Trust me, he's gonna fucking talk."

"Hey, Alex?" Kaden's voice became softer.

"Yes?"

"You really care about her, don't you?"

The brunette closed her eyes and sighed before she answered. "Yes."

"Cool. I've gotta go, one of the nurses just entered his room."

He ended the call and Alex removed the phone from her ear. She blankly stared down at it as her thoughts seemed to swarm her mind.

"Are you okay?" croaked a voice behind her. Alex felt her heart jump and she spun around to the direction she heard the voice. Avery sat up in the bed, eyes tired as her fingers scratched behind Milo's ear. The small dog's tail wagged violently as he licked around her face, happy his owner was okay.

"Avery," the taller girl breathed out with a smile. "I should be asking you the same question."

The freckled girl frowned and shrugged as she seemed to remember the events that triggered her panic attack. "I'm alright."

Alex's eyebrows came together in concern as she made a move to stand up. "I should go tell Carson and your parents that you're awake." This caused Avery to shake her head fervently. She reached out her hand and wrapped it around Alex's wrist in an attempt to stop her.

"No, don't go," her voice cracked. With her other hand, she patted the space next to her on the bed. "Stay."

"Freckles, they're concerned for you. We all are."

Avery's hand gripped Alex's wrist, "Please."

Alex nodded her head hesitantly before crawling over to the space that Avery had set aside for her. Once she had properly sat down and adjusted herself under the covers, she felt a weight on her shoulder. When she looked down, she noticed that the shorter girl had rested her head there as she played with the small dog on her lap. The brunette felt a slight blush rise to her cheeks.

"What did you tell Carson?" she asked softly. Alex wrapped an arm around Avery's waist, pulling her closer to her side. She didn't know where the urge came from.

"That I had invited you over so you could tutor me in French and that the session went overtime so you were there at the same time as the boys. Sam said some mean things and you had a panic attack."

Avery was silent for a while before the feeling of something wet dripping down her arm brought Alex's attention downwards once more. Avery sniffled and used the back of her hand to wipe her eyes.

"I just don't want to lose him," Avery whispered as her breaths came out shakily, "but I don't want to lose you either."

"Hey," Alex said seriously. She placed her fingers underneath Avery's chin and brought her head up so they were at eye level. Just as she did before, she used her thumbs to wipe away the tears that escaped from her eyes. "No matter what happens, I promise, you're not going to lose me."

Avery smiled and let out a chuckle through her tears. "You're such an amazing friend. Thank you."

Alex laughed a little as well, "You're not so bad yourself, Freckles."

Now that they were this close without Avery being in potential danger, Alex was able to observe the small details of her face. She allowed her eyes to run over every freckle and every beauty mark on her skin. She appreciated the term 'beauty mark' because they really were marks of beauty that rested on the face of her friend.

She was able to admire Avery's brown eyes. She had never expected to find brown eyes so interesting. There were no specks of gold or blue or green; they were just wholly brown, but they were gorgeous just the same. They were complemented by a nice set of long lashes which were a bit clumped together by the moisture of her tears, but it only accentuated its length and beauty.

Her eyes went to her lips, a little dry and a mix between brown and pink. She imagined they were soft because that's how Avery was, everything about her was smooth and soft. She felt her thumb unconsciously trace over her cupid's bow as she followed the line with her gaze. The freckled girl's bottom lip was plumper than the top one, and at that moment all Alex could think of was how it would feel between her teeth.

Hesitantly, she leaned towards Avery until they were mere two or three inches apart causing the other girl to chuckle nervously. "What are you doing?" Avery whispered, trying to look anywhere but Alex's eyes. She felt the brunette place a soft kiss to her nose before resuming her former position. The kiss was quick and chaste but it brought a blush to her face.

"Oh-" she wasn't able to finish before her lips were captured by Alex's. After the initial shock, she felt her heart soar. The kiss lasted just as long as the one to her nose and when Alex drew back, Avery felt her chest build up with a world of emotions.

Alex licked her lips as she looked at the freckled girl again. She was right, Avery was nothing but smooth and soft. With a rapidly beating heart, Avery sat up and made eye contact with the brunette in front of her. Her fingers wrapped around her forearms and brought Alex in for a continuation of what had just occurred.

Alex's hand went to the small of Avery's back, pulling her in as close as possible. As the two relished in the feel of having each other's lips against their own, Avery's hands moved to the back of Alex's neck before she felt the taller girl use her tongue to prod at her lips.

Avery didn't know much about kissing, in fact, this was her first kiss- well, now her second. But, she had read books and watched movies, so she had a hint of what to do. She parted her lips, allowing Alex's tongue to enter her mouth and earning a soft groan of appreciation from the brunette.

Alex had never felt this way just kissing someone before. She felt happy, she felt content, she felt full. She wanted to bring the girl in her arms even closer, though it was impossible.

She detached their lips, wanting to keep things 'PG' because it was their first time and hopefully not their last. She placed a small kiss to the shorter girl's forehead and then moved down to her cheeks, attempting to cover every single freckle with an individual kiss. When she pulled back, Avery's cheeks were pink and she seemed dazed.

Alex was the first to speak, a smirk blossoming on her features. "I should bring you down to your parents."

Chapter 14

The start of the school week had Avery's head in a frenzy. So many things had changed and she felt anxious as she walked down the hallway to her locker. She had to avoid Sam who, like Alex and the others, was popular and it proved not to be an easy feat. Plus, she and Alex had recently kissed and Avery had no idea where it left them in regards to their friendship, but she knew she still had to keep it a secret from Carson who had now become increasingly overprotective.

Maybe she was being irrational, keeping it from him? She wished nothing more than to gush to her best friend about her first kiss but found herself unable to and it was her own fault. What had started out to be simply an omission of information had now become a web of lies and fabricated stories including the events from the weekend. One might recall that Avery was not the best at planning things out and frankly, the fact came to bite her in the ass.

"Hey," a voice sounded next to Avery's ear. Avery reluctantly looked over, anticipating it to be one of the many people she was trying to avoid. She figured that maybe if she just evaded Sam, Kaden, Jason, Alex and Carson everything would be okay...temporarily. She let out an audible sigh of relief when she saw that the person walking next to her was only Marigold.

"Hey."

"I just wanted to thank you for talking to Carson," Marigold smiled warmly at the freckled girl. When she took notice of her confused expression, she elaborated, "Carson asked me out over the weekend. I've liked him for a while now and I know that he wouldn't have made a move without asking for your blessing. So, thank you."

"Oh," Avery replied simply as she stopped in front of her locker, causing the redhead to do the same. "I think you guys would be good for each other," she added with a shaky smile, trying to push away the negative thoughts that came forth as she said those words. Her subconscious was trying to remind her that when Carson finds out she's been lying to him, Marigold will be her replacement. She could only attempt to postpone that future as far as possible.

The athletic redhead placed a hand on her shoulder, evoking a startled jump from the freckled girl. If Marigold had noticed her strange reaction, she didn't show it as her face turned serious, "I just want you to know that I don't hold it against you, the way you treated me. I understand that you're just looking out for your best friend."

Avery frowned. Maybe she was just paranoid because of what's happening in her life, but Marigold's words seemed almost accusatory. Like she did hold it against her. If she hadn't then she wouldn't have brought it up, right?

She plastered on a smile. "Carson and I always have each other's back. It's what we do."

Marigold patted the shoulder that her hand still rested on and smiled brightly once more, "I've gotta go. I'll see you at lunch."

After she waved goodbye to Marigold, Avery quickly put the books she needed into her backpack and closed her locker once she remembered that Carson was her locker neighbour. It would explain why Marigold knew where to find her. The redhead's locker was nowhere close to that area and she had never shown any real interest in Avery anyway. That was most likely the freckled girl's own fault. Not only did she screw up her chances with her current best friend, but she screwed up her chance at making a new one too.

Avery pulled her sweater's hoodie over her head and drew its drawstrings, tightening it around her face. She just wanted to disappear at the moment. She had become less and less of a wallflower lately and wished she could just revert to the way her life was before. Everything was so complicated now. Before, the most she had to worry about was homework, whether her mom was baking cookies, whether she brought her umbrella with her as to not get caught in the rain and avoiding anxiety attacks. She wasn't built for drama.

Her first class of the morning was Physics and she briskly walked towards the direction of the designated classroom. Her path was constantly obstructed by the many students who attended her school and so she found herself winding and swerving to get around them, occasionally brushing shoulders with one or two people.

While rushing to her classroom she bumped into a soft chest, head-on. The coconut smell that enveloped her was a telltale sign as to who it was and she felt her heart rate spike. She shoved her hands in her pockets and ducked her head down, attempting to sidestep Alex. Before she could walk away, the brunette grabbed her arm and pulled her back.

"Freckles," she called to her, but Avery remained silent and looked to the ground as if it was the most interesting thing in the world. Alex tried again, "Freckles."

The taller girl was surprised and though she hated to admit it, kind of hurt. She had always been the one to ghost the girls she hooked up with but never had she herself been ghosted. Especially by someone she had actual feelings for and hadn't even hooked up with.

"I have to get to class," Avery mumbled under her breath, trying to pry herself from Alex's grasp. She didn't want to but she felt like she had to. Being around Alex now made her feel guilty and reminded her of her current situation with Carson; the fact that she was lying to him. Her attempts were to no avail as the brunette kept an iron grip on her arm, firm enough to keep her rooted in the spot but gentle enough not to hurt her. For a brief second, Avery's mind wandered to what Alex possibly does to get so strong before snapping herself out of her thoughts.

"The bell hasn't even rung yet." Alex's voice was soft as she spoke to her. She placed her fingers under Avery's chin and loosened the drawstrings before tilting the shorter girl's head upwards, forcing her to look her in the eyes. She didn't know if she should bring up the fact that Avery was blatantly avoiding her and hadn't responded to her messages since the day everything happened, but it was bothering her.

Using her free hand, Avery swatted away Alex's hand from her chin once she noticed that other students had stopped to view their encounter. The brunette narrowed her eyes at the freckled girl who felt guilt nip at her.

"I have to go," Avery muttered quickly, trying once again to free herself. She didn't expect Alex to pull her by her arm, dragging her as she walked hastily through the hallway. Her actions drew the attention of many of the students that they passed and Avery felt as if she wanted to die, cheeks turning pink from embarrassment. It probably looked as if she was a child, about to get scolded by her mother.

Once they had reached what Avery assumed was their destination, Alex lightly pushed her, making her stumble inside an empty classroom. The taller girl stepped inside after her and locked the door.

"What are you doing?" Avery asked, voice sounding tired.

"What am I doing? What are you doing?" Alex rebutted, frustration evident in her tone. When the curly-haired girl didn't respond, her eyes softened. Alex sighed deeply, deciding to cut to the chase, "Why are you avoiding me, Avery?"

The use of her actual name stung and Avery flinched. Why was she messing everything up?

"I'm not," she started and then paused, "Okay, I am."

"Did I do something wrong?" Alex took a step closer, causing Avery to take a step backwards.

"No."

"I'm finding that hard to believe," Alex deadpanned.

It was Avery's time to sigh before she confessed, "You didn't do anything wrong and that's the problem. It's me. I'm doing everything wrong." She felt her throat getting tight and stopped talking.

"I don't understand," the brunette took a step forward again, and this time Avery let her.

"I like you, Alex. If it wasn't obvious," the freckled girl confessed, feeling a blush rise to her cheeks. "But now that my feelings are clear to me and after...what we did... I feel guilty. I feel guilty about lying to Carson, but I can't tell him now. He'll hate me. I feel like une connasse. I just want things to go back to normal. I don't even know if you and I are friends anymore, something more, or if that what we had was just a pity kiss." {Bitch/Shit-head/Asshole}

"Trust me," Alex took another step forward, "it wasn't a pity kiss."

"It wasn't?"

Alex rubbed the back of her neck sheepishly, "I feel the same way about you, actually. I have ever since you sneezed on me."

If Avery wasn't feeling so terrible at the moment, she would have teased her about the blush that twinged her ears and cheeks.

Alex continued as she took another step forward, "And remember what I told you- no matter what, you won't lose me. I don't know what to say that will ease your mind about Carson, but I want you to know that I'm here for you."

She was right, her words didn't ease her mind but they at least brought a smile to her face. She took this moment to tease her, "What happened to the bad person I used to know?"

Alex smirked down at her, "She doesn't like you very much so she tends not to be here when you are."

Avery put a hand to her chest and pouted, "I'm wounded."

The brunette used a hand to cup her cheek as they continued to banter, "Coincidentally, she had just wanted to stab you to solve the problem but I convinced her not to."

"My hero."

Alex finally brought their lips together in a tender kiss and once more, Avery felt her heart soar. It was crazy

that someone could make her feel like this without doing much. The two embraced each other as they both
tried to express their emotion in a way that words could
not.

Tired of standing on her tiptoes to meet the taller girl
halfway, Avery wrapped her arms around her neck in
an attempt to pull her down further as the kiss became
more passionate. Not willing to bend so far down, Alex
gripped her thighs and lifted her up effortlessly before
walking them over to the nearest desk. Her actions
evoked a squeak from Avery which was quickly muffled
by the brunette's mouth. She placed Avery on the table
to sit and stood between her legs, still gently cupping
them.

Avery had never done anything like this before in her
life, but she loved it. Reluctantly, she pulled away from
Alex to catch her breath.

"This is not how I saw my morning going," Avery joked,
almost panting. Seeing her freckled friend so flushed
and with swollen lips made Alex lick her lips and dip her
head down, once more capturing her lips.

Suddenly, the bell rang startling Avery and bringing
her to part from Alex once more.

"Merde," she clutched her chest, heart pounding. The
taller girl internally groaned at their parting, wanting
to bring them together once more. She bit her swollen

bottom lip as she looked down at the girl in front of her who was still trying to steady her heartbeat. Avery's use of French was not helping her case.

Her hands still rested on Avery's thighs and she used them to draw the shorter girl closer. Alex's actions did nothing for Avery's quickening heart rate as she wondered to herself whether or not it was possible for someone to be so attractive. But she definitely wasn't complaining. She couldn't even wrap her head around the fact that she was seated on a desk in an empty classroom, legs wrapped around the school's bad girl after just making out with her. It was so out of character.

"Skip class with me," Alex pleaded, but her now raspy voice and natural suave made it seem more like a command.

"To do what? More of this?"

"Only if you want to, but that's not what I had in mind," the brunette's intentions weren't to sleep with her so quickly. She genuinely found Avery to be a fascinating young woman and wanted to spend more of her time with her. She was also very respectful of Avery's boundaries.

Avery looked dubious, "I don't skip class."

Alex's thumb brushed over her bottom lip before giving it a small peck. She then shifted her head to Avery's ear and whispered sending a shiver down the shorter girl's spine, "Come on Freckles."

"Okay."

Avery cursed herself for giving in so quickly. Sure their feelings were now out in the open but she didn't want to make it seem like she was thirsty for the first girl that walked past.

"Okay?" the brunette smirked.

Avery nodded, "Okay," she confirmed.

Alex stepped backwards and offered the freckled girl a helping hand in getting down from the desk. She waited patiently and observed as Avery adjusted and smoothed out her sweater, removed the hoodie from her head and fixed her hair.

"Are you ready?" she asked now that the shorter girl had finished.

"Let's go."

Chapter 15

"Avery Carine Toussaint!" Avery heard as soon as she stepped through her front door. She looked up after she wiped her boots on the welcome mat. The light snow from the weekend had somewhat melted and turned to sludge on the streets, leaving her boots dirty and wet. Her mother stood in the doorway of the kitchen, hands on her hips in her traditional scolding style.

"Maman?" Avery's eyebrows furrowed in confusion, removing her boots and coat so she could step towards her mother.

"Why did I get a call from your school saying that you left campus this morning and never came back?" her mother's eyes narrowed as she looked at her. Avery's heart rate quickened and she looked to the floor. She and Alex had gone out for frozen yoghurt and the brunette drove her to a scenic spot on a hilltop where they just sat and talked.

And kissed.

But only a little.

They had never meant to miss the whole day of school, only a class or two, and now Avery was left wracking her brain for a reasonable excuse.

" Dîtes-moi," her mom pushed. Her tone was stern and the freckled girl couldn't bear to look her in the eyes and face the disappointment that could be there. She wasn't one to get in trouble regularly- if at all. {Tell me}

In order to get her mother off her case, she felt herself blurt out, "I had an anxiety attack at school and I wasn't feeling so well afterwards. I left school to try to calm myself down. I just couldn't go back, maman. J'suis désolée." {I'm sorry}

She had never lied about her anxiety before and she almost felt horrible about it, but she was somewhat still walking on clouds from her time spent with Alex. Her mother's stance relaxed and her facial features contorted to one of concern and she rushed forward and enveloped her daughter in her arms.

"Oh Doux-Doux, why didn't you just come home?"

"I was with my friend. She was concerned for me so she stuck with me," Avery's lie continued. She seemed to be doing a lot of lying lately.

Her daughter's confession brought Mrs Toussaint to lift her head and look at her daughter, "Which friend?"

"Alex. Remember you met her when we got Milo."

"Oh. The tall, pretty girl with the very long hair?"

Avery fought the urge to blush and instead rolled her eyes; Alex's hair really was amazing. It was a pity she didn't wear it down more often. She couldn't help but wonder if Alex would wear it down if she asked her to.

"Maman, you've only met two of my friends."

"You have others?" Her mother half-joked.

"Yes," the freckled girl said, but it came out more like a question. She wasn't sure if she'd consider Marigold a friend and she had only just met Kaden and Jason. Mrs Toussaint only rolled her eyes and decided to change the subject, "Je ne t'ai pas vu prendre tes médicaments ce matin. Take them and then go shower." {I didn't see you take your medicine this morning}

If there was one thing that Avery's mother was good at, it was disciplining her child. It came as second nature due to her Congolese upbringing but unlike her own parents, she knew where to draw the line between dictator and confidant. Avery was able to grow up knowing not to get herself in trouble while also knowing not to fear her parents.

"D'accord."

The curly-haired girl headed up the stairwell when she felt her phone vibrate. She bit the inside of her cheek when she read the name of the sender and almost tripped on the way to her room. After closing her room door and greeting Milo, she flopped down on the soft bed that seemed to have been waiting for her, the small dog jumping up as well to lay on her chest.

Avery unlocked her phone hastily and went to her conversation with Alex.

Alex: Did you get home safe?

It was just a question but somehow it meant the world to Avery and she felt her face break out into a wide grin. She had read all sorts of books, including cheesy romance novels, but she had always assumed that the authors were exaggerating in the ways they described falling for someone. She was starting to learn that that wasn't the case.

A: I did. My maman was a bit upset at first but she's good now. How about you?

Alex: I'm still on the road... at Jason's house.

Alex: What did you say to her? Does she hate me even more now?

Avery knew that Alex was referring to Mrs Toussaint's attitude towards her when they had first met. It was understandable why the brunette would think that her mother hated her, but she was always overprotective and never had been good at first impressions.

A: Oh hush, she doesn't hate you. I told her I had an anxiety attack and had to leave and you followed me to help calm me down. She seemed happy with that.

A: Also she says you have nice hair.

Alex: Oh, lying to the 'rents now are we?

The freckled girl could somehow feel Alex's smirk through the phone, but she didn't know how to respond. She knew the brunette was only teasing but she couldn't help the guilt that nipped at her once more.

A: It was a one-time thing.

Alex: Okay.

Avery's hands fell from their previous position where they once held her phone up as she typed. She let them flop down beside her with a sigh and her phone slide out from her fingertips. Milo yipped at his owner as if he could sense the shift in her mood. With light steps, he came off of her chest and walked over to her head, sliding his tongue up her cheek in an affectionate kiss.

"Hey, Milo," Avery giggled before flipping over to her stomach, scratching the puppy behind his ears. She spent a while playing with the pup and rubbing his belly before she figured it was time for her to go take a bath. Grabbing her essentials, including a bath bomb, from her drawers she headed over to her bathroom.

She didn't have an ensuite, though she had begged for it multiple times, yet she was lucky enough to have a bathroom that was situated right next to her bedroom. Plus, being an only child meant she had it all to herself.

Avery placed all her things on the flat area by her bath-tub and turned on the water. She let it run, occasionally testing to see if it was warm enough. When she was satisfied with the water level, she dropped in her bath bomb and afterwards slowly lowered herself into the inviting water which was now a mint green colour. The only thing she was missing now was music.

She reached over and opened her phone, turning on a custom-made Spotify playlist and allowed the smooth music to fill the room. Avery's music taste had always leaned toward more soft and relaxing music, sometimes acoustic and sometimes with low beats. After she had scrubbed herself with a loofah, she closed her eyes and sunk deeper into the warm water, letting it wet the hair that was now down to her shoulders.

Avery was almost asleep when she heard her mother's voice call her from downstairs. Startled by the sudden noise, she sat up quickly and knocked some of her bath gels into the tub in the process.

"Avery, quelqu'une est là pour te voir!" Mrs Toussaint yelled from downstairs. {Someone is here to see you}

Avery groaned long and loud as she dipped her head under the water, wanting to get back to the state of peace she was in only seconds ago. Who would come to visit her at her house?

Her blood ran cold at the realisation of the only person who came to mind. She knew she couldn't turn Carson away, because that way he would know for sure that something was going on. Then he'd be suspicious because Avery had never avoided him before.

With a shaky voice, Avery called out, "Send them up, maman!"

"Merde," she cursed to herself, getting out of the bathtub and quickly drying herself off with a towel. What would she say to him? How would she explain why he hadn't seen her in so long? (Long being relative in this context).

Avery wrapped the towel around her body and let the water drain from the sink. She gathered the things she had brought to the bathroom and slipped on her fuzzy slippers before opening the door.

When she stepped out, she scurried into her room and closed the door quickly, letting out a sigh. She squeezed her eyes closed and felt her mind swarm with scenarios and multiple outcomes of how her encounter with Carson might turn out.

"Um," Avery heard a voice say and she let out a scream as her eyes snapped open. All her toiletries fell to the floor and she nearly lost hold of her towel because sitting on her bed with Milo in their lap was Alex Rivers.

"C'est quoi ce bordel?" she groaned, once her heart rate slowed down to the pace it was at before. {What the fuck?}

"Hi," Alex said awkwardly, averting her gaze with a blush. Her hand went to the back of her head where she rubbed her neck sheepishly. Avery couldn't help but think that that was such an adorable habit she had whenever she felt nervous or awkward. Snapping herself out of her thoughts, Avery cleared her throat and clutched her towel even tighter.

"Hey Alex. What are you doing here?"

Though she so desperately wanted to look, the brunette kept her stare on the floor in order to give Avery the privacy she needed. "I wanted to apologize for what I said on the phone. I didn't mean to sound insensitive."

A moment of silence passed between them as Avery observed the tall girl. Finally, she spoke, "So let me get this straight. You left your friend's house to come to mine because you thought that something you texted sounded insensitive?" Avery felt her heart melt. If it was somehow possible, she felt she would have turned into a puddle at that moment when Alex nodded, eyes still trained on the floor.

"Mon Dieu, je t'adore beaucoup," Avery whispered to herself as her heart pounded in her ears. Her stomach was almost nauseous with butterflies. {God, I like you a lot}

"Moi aussi," Alex responded. She was a puddle. The freckled girl definitely swore she was a puddle at this point. {Me too}

"What?"

"It means 'me too'-" Alex started to explain nervously, almost on the verge of rambling before Avery cut her off. She loved seeing her this way. Knowing that the well guarded and badass popular girl could let down her walls around her.

"I, obviously, know what it means. But, how do you know what it means?" Avery asked, walking towards her, forgetting all about the fact that she was in a towel. In fact, the brunette almost forgot too as she glanced up at the shorter girl and looked back down.

"I started learning French thanks to Duolingo," she replied with a small chuckle.

"I could just kiss you right now. Who knew Alexia Rivers was such a romantic?"

"And who knew Avery Toussaint was so bold?" Alex teased back, correctly pronouncing Avery's last name this time, which the freckled girl took notice of. She also noticed that Alex didn't correct her when she called her Alexia.

"You're rubbing off on me," Avery spoke before grabbing the back of Alex's head with a free hand and bringing it to hers. Her fingers weaved through the taller girl's hair as they kissed sweetly.

"You probably shouldn't say that while you're only in a towel, love," Alex smirked when they parted.

"Perv," the freckled girl said with a laugh.

Alex allowed her eyes to glance up and down Avery's body teasingly, "I mean, can you blame me?"

Avery took a step back, a blush and sheepish smile on her face, "I'm gonna go change."

The brunette looked up from one of Avery's books with a smile once the shorter girl re-entered the room from her closet. One needs not to point out the irony in the situation.

"I like this outfit," Alex commented appreciatively before she dropped the book, tugging Avery's hand as soon as she got close enough. She had changed into a black long-sleeved shirt underneath a green pinafore. The taller girl placed a small peck to her lips once she sat next to her on the bed.

"Only because this is your favourite shade of green," Avery responded, gesturing to the emerald green of her pinafore. She and Alex had very different senses of style. The curly-haired girl usually stuck to more preppy clothing while the brunette wore more laid-back and sometimes edgy clothes.

"Not necessarily. I always like everything you wear," Alex said nonchalantly, now lying on her side, head resting on her palm. Her fingers laced themselves with Avery's and played with her fingertips.

"Thank you for coming over," Avery sighed happily, her free hand playing with Milo.

"Go out with me," the brunette blurted abruptly, cheeks and nose pink. "On a date."

Avery's head turned slightly to look Alex in the eye, eyebrows set in confusion. Her green eyes shone beautifully with desperation -something Avery wasn't sure if she'd ever seen in Alex's eyes before.

"We went out earlier today," the curly-haired girl reminded, not understanding what Alex was trying to ask.

"That was just us spending time together. Nothing official."

"Isn't that what a date is?" she teased, almost immediately sobered up by the brunette's unimpressed look. "I'd love to go on an official date with you," she admitted, bringing a smile to Alex's face that reached her eyes. She placed a chaste kiss on her lips.

"I've got to go," Alex noted after her eyes caught the analogue clock that was hung up on the wall of Avery's room.

"Already?" the freckled girl's head lifted from the bed head as she sat up.

"This was supposed to be just a quick visit, but you're too hypnotising," Avery's cheeks heated at the comment. "I have to do some stuff for my mom and step-dad before they get home."

The brunette got up from the bed and placed a kiss on the top of Milo's head. The puppy had certainly grown on her.

"I'll see you on Wednesday at seven. I'll pick you up, wear something casual," she then placed a kiss to Avery's nose.

"Wait, but that's two days away," Avery said hurriedly. Alex's leaving was so abrupt she felt like she was in a rush to keep up with her. "Let me walk you out."

Alex placed a kiss to her lips, longer than the kiss they had before, evoking a content sigh from Avery. The two exited the room and walked downstairs.

Mrs Toussaint rose from her seat in the living room sofa once she saw the two young women appear. Just like Alex and Milo, the brunette was starting to grow on her too. She saw that she had been there for her daughter when they had bought Milo, when she brought Avery home after her panic attack and how she comforted her daughter when she left school earlier today. She also paid attention to the spark she put in Avery's eye and how the freckled girl had seemed to come out of her shell a little bit more. Mrs Toussaint assumed that the reason Alex had visited their home was to check up on Avery after this morning and that gave her yet another point in her book.

"Bonsoir, madame," Alex bid goodbye to Avery's mother, giving her a handshake after she took notice that the woman was not necessarily fond of physical contact from those who weren't her immediate family.

"Bye, Freckles," the brunette smiled warmly at the shorter girl, giving her hand a gentle and reassuring squeeze before they parted ways.

Mother and daughter stood by the doorway, watching as the tall girl got into her car and headed out the driveway. Once the cold air had nipped enough at their feet, Mrs Toussaint closed the front door and turned to Avery.

"Quelle douce fille," she commented to the freckled girl who was in somewhat of a trance as she thought about Alex. The visit was way too short for her liking and left her head and heart in a dilly. {What a sweet girl}

Avery nodded absentmindedly in agreement and spoke what had meant to be a thought, "I like her so much."

Chapter 16

"Where have you been?" Carson closed Avery's locker, seeming to suddenly appear out of nowhere. The freckled girl jumped in her spot and held her books to her chest.

"In class," she responded slowly, deciding to play coy. Technically, it wasn't a fib; she really had been in class all day. Her friend's lips tugged down into a slight frown as he looked on at her.

"Stop," he said tiredly, reaching out his hand to lay on her shoulder, "You know what I mean. The last time we spoke you came out to me, then you had a panic attack later on. I'm concerned for you Aves."

When she didn't respond and kept her eyes trained on her shoes, he continued, "Did you tell your parents and they didn't take it so well? If that's the case then you can talk to me, we're best friends. I'll be here for you no matter what."

Hearing Carson's words of compassion made her feel even worse about her situation. How did she even end up in this mess? Why didn't she just tell the truth from the beginning?

It was like a dam had burst and tears fell from her eyes, cascading down her cheeks and eventually dripping onto the tiled floor.

Avery had so badly just wanted to say 'I've been lying to you. Alex and I are dating and I don't tutor her in French. I had a panic attack because one of her friends called me out. I'm a horrible person and I don't deserve you'. So she did because she couldn't take the guilt and pain anymore.

Avery told him everything.

Right there, in the middle of the hallway. Heart beating too fast and mind racing too quickly to pay attention to the peers that had crowded around them.

She watched as his face contorted into different expressions as she revealed the whole story, exposed the omissions and clarified the lies. When she was done, the new expression on his face was almost unreadable, but what was written in his eyes was a look she'd never forget. Pain. And it was all her fault. She was the one causing him this pain.

Her high from yesterday evening came crashing down.

"So how long has this been going on for?" he cleared his throat after he asked his question, but Avery didn't miss the crack in his voice when he did.

"Early November," she whispered. That was the day when she and Alex had gone to get Milo and the brunette had learned about her anxiety disorder, jump-starting their friendship.

"It's the middle of December now," he said, mainly to himself. He was still trying to wrap his head around the fact that his best friend had been lying to him for about a month now. She was getting close to someone she knew he wouldn't have approved of and tried to cover it up. Carson and Alex were popular (albeit for different reasons), which meant they saw each other at parties and bonfires and occasionally spoke to each other. He had never known Alex to be girlfriend material; she had had many suitors but would never hold on to one.

If Avery had come to him about her feelings then he could have told her that and advised her not to get romantically involved with someone like Alex. But she didn't. Instead, she lied to him. He wouldn't have gone through the trouble of asking the freckled girl for her blessing of his relationship with Marigold if he had known that Avery didn't care enough to do the same.

It made him wonder. How many other things could she have been lying to him about? Carson had never thought Avery to be capable of keeping a lie going for so long to anybody, much more himself. But people, they can surprise you.

Carson wanted nothing more than to forgive her, swing his arm over the shoulder of the now crying girl, like he normally did, and walk her to her class. But Avery had taught him, when it came to his failed relationships, not to allow people to just walk over his heart and let them back in.

"We're best friends. Practically siblings," he reiterated. "We tell each other everything and you lied to me."

The volume of Avery's sobs only increased and her legs felt weak.

"You didn't even trust me enough to forgive you. You thought I was going to leave you. I think that's the part that hurts most. The guilt you feel is nothing compared to the pain I do."

With that, he left Avery leaning against her locker for support. Her world felt like it was falling apart. The inquisitive students, who had gathered around the pair of best friends to listen in to the situation, were now gossiping amongst each other. They looked at her with faces of disappointment, malice, disgust and annoyance- not that she had expected anything different.

Gone was her previous wallflower status. She was now known as the girl who broke Carson Armani's heart.

Chapter 17

A very had had to be removed from her position on the floor of the school hallways, where she sat and stared at the tiles. She had run out of tears to cry and the only thing that came out was the occasional hiccup. The bell had long rung and the corridors were so silent and empty, she could hear a pin drop.

She had heard the approaching footsteps after the second bell had rung, but did nothing to fight off the hands that carried her to the nurse's office.

And there she sat, Alex to one side and Jason to the next. Her hair was wild from previously running her hands through them and her stare was blank. It was like she had shut down completely and was almost unresponsive to what was happening around her.

"Do either of you two know her personally?" the nurse asked, words drawn out and tone uncaring like she had done this millions of times before.

"I do," Alex spoke up. Her fingers were itching to intertwine themselves with Avery's but she didn't know how the shorter girl would feel about the public display affection, especially in her state.

"Does she have any sicknesses or illnesses I should know about?" the woman looked up over her clipboard, a bored expression adorned on her features.

"She has General Anxiety disorder, but she's taking Zoloft for it."

The nurse scribbled something down on a piece of paper and handed it to the brunette, not giving the curly-haired girl on the bed a second glance. She pointed to the nurse's pass now in Alex's hand, "Here, take her home."

"That's it? Is that even allowed? Shouldn't you do something like give her a check-up? See what's wrong?" Alex asked, voice raising as she clutched the note in her hand.

The grown woman turned her head to face the brunette on her way out to another section of the office, "Since when do you care about what's allowed, Alex Rivers?"

****

"I can't believe he would do that to her," Alex gritted out as she gripped the steering wheel tighter. Jason only shook his head in the passenger seat, eyes focused on the road ahead. The brunette was close to passing the speed limit due to the rage that pumped through her body.

"In front of the whole fucking school, no less. He knows she hates crowds," she continued, "We weren't even there, but yet we heard about it right after it happened. Can you imagine the emotional trauma she went through? That asshole was her rock."

Alex's eyes flitted up to the rearview mirror to get a glance at the freckled girl. Avery's eyelids were closed now, it was unknown to the brunette whether she was sleeping or whether she had just decided to tune everything out.

"I'm gonna fucking kill him," she gritted out in lowly, her knuckles were now white and her fingernails were pressed into the leather coating of the steering wheel.

"No," Jason spoke, "If you hurt him, you hurt her. He may be upset, but she still cares about him."

When Alex pulled into the Toussaint's driveway, she let out a deep sigh and turned towards her best friend in the seat next to her. "Thanks for coming with me. Could you stay in the car while I bring her up? You might give her mother a scare," she said, hinting towards Jason's intimidating nature and abundance of tattoos, "You can run the heater while I'm gone. If I take too long you can always head to my house or yours, I can pick up the car later."

The well-built young man gave a quick nod and started the car again once Alex stepped out. The tall girl walked towards the backseat and opened the door.

"Freckles," she nudged her shoulder before picking up a caramel hand and pressing it to her lips. Avery slowly opened her eyes in response.

"I'm gonna carry you into your house okay? But you have to wrap an arm around my shoulder," she said with a comforting smile, adjusting the smaller girl in her arms in preparation to carry her bridal style. Avery sluggishly followed her instructions after giving a hesitant nod. Alex was just happy she had received some type of response.

After the freckled girl was securely in her arms, she walked to the front door and used the finger of one of the hands that gripped her to rap on the door. Only a few moments later did it open to reveal a dishevelled Mrs Toussaint with flour in her coily hair. The woman had a smile on her face which had now disappeared with a gasp once she saw her daughter in Alex's arms.

"Mon Dieu! Come in, come in," she gestured hurriedly with one of her hands, using the other to open the door wider.

"She's more or less fine...physically. She had a very emotional morning," the brunette decided to fill in the doting mother who nodded in understanding.

"Would you be able to put her upstairs in her room? You look like an athletic young lady. Once you've done that, come down and let's talk. I'll put out some cookies for you."

Gently, the brunette brought the freckled girl to her bedroom upstairs. During her ascent she occasionally looked down at her face to see if she was alright, only to be met with the same blank stare. After she had opened the door, she gently placed Avery on the well-made queen-sized bed. She adjusted the covers so that the shorter girl was wrapped up underneath them, just in case she got cold and placed a small kiss to her forehead.

"I'm just gonna be downstairs, okay? I'm still here," she said in an attempt to reassure her. Avery nodded faintly in reply and mustered up enough energy to send the brunette a quick smile.

Alex gave Avery's hand one last quick squeeze before she headed down the stairs, making sure to leave the bedroom door ajar.

"What happened?" Mrs Toussaint's concerned voice sounded from the kitchen once she heard the tall girl's footsteps approach her. She exited soon afterwards with a tray of cookies in her hand and placed them on a small round table. Using her hand, she gestured for Alex to sit across from her, only the white glass table separating the pair.

"Oh I almost forgot, would you like something to drink? Avery usually has her cookies with milk. Should I get you the same?"

The brunette shook her head and stopped herself before Mrs Toussaint could notice. Where were her manners? "No, thank you. Water should be fine, please."

Soon enough, the ebony woman returned with a glass water and placed it on the table. She folded her arms expectedly on her lap and looked at Alex, waiting for her to reveal the details of the morning's occurrence.

"I wasn't there to see it all go down, but she and Carson had a very public... falling out. He told her off a bit and the school turned against her. Armani's the golden boy, so of course, the school population would rally behind him. I guess it was too much for Avery to handle and I found her on the floor in the same spot by her locker where everything happened."

Mrs Toussaint let out a deep sigh and shook her head, "She shut down. She used to do that when she was younger. All the emotions are too overwhelming and so her brain finds a way to protect her. It's like she dissociates." When she saw the concerned look on Alex's face as she twiddled with her thumbs she continued, "It doesn't last long, don't worry. Normally it takes about an hour or two for her to be back. It happens with the anxiety; it's a way for her to cope."

When the brunette didn't comment, the woman pondered to herself, "Those two are as thick as thieves. I wonder what could have happened between them to cause this."

Alex had to bite her tongue before she spewed some indecent choice words about Carson, so she took a deep breath in. "You'd have to ask Avery about that, madame."

An awkward silence settled quickly between them and the tall girl was itching to get up and check on Avery. Mrs Toussaint stared at the glass table and Alex instinctively bit into a chocolate chip cookie.

"This is very good," Alex complimented in an attempt to ease the tension. The grown woman nodded in acknowledgement.

"I think you make her very happy," she said silently, almost in a whisper. If Alex was a bit more distracted, she doubted she would have even heard the words that left her mouth.

"I hope so. She deserves happiness."

"I think so too," Mrs Toussaint paused before deciding to address the elephant in the room, despite Alex's not knowing that there was one. "Yesterday she told me she likes you. I don't think she meant to say it so I didn't comment on it. But tell me, are you in a romantic or platonic relationship with my daughter?"

Alex shifted uncomfortably in her seat, her eyes darting to the corners of the room. This was not the conversation she thought she would have been having at this moment. She knew she couldn't say the whole 'you'd have to ask Avery' thing again. That would leave Avery's mother feeling annoyed and she could be rather intimidating.

"I mean..." she trailed off, not knowing how to answer. "Things are very new."

"Things are new, but the feelings are not," Mrs Toussaint chimed in intuitively. The brunette only nodded. "I guess I should allow her to come out to me and her father first before I ask any more questions. I just hope she trusts us enough."

"I'm sure she will."

"What was it like when you came out to your parents?" the woman asked, leaning forward with interest. Her eyes went wide before she tried to correct herself. "If you came out to your parents." Her eyes went even wider, "Mon Dieu, if you even have parents."

Alex was left chuckling lightly at Mrs Toussaint's fumbling, it reminded her so much of her freckled girl. She could tell that the woman wasn't used to conversations like these. "Yes, I have parents," she reaffirmed, "My mom handled it pretty well when I came out, but my dad didn't. So he left. The reality of having a daughter who's a lesbian was too surreal for him to hang around his family, so he bounced."

"I'm sorry to hear."

"Yeah well, we don't really miss him much and for the past two years my mom has been in a way happier marriage."

"Hm," she hummed in thought. "Phillipe is pretty openminded, so there won't be any problems there. In regards to Avery shutting down, I might have to call Dr Rosenburg and ask him to move up their next appointment."

"Sounds like Avery is in good hands then," Alex said with a smile, finally feeling like she could breathe again once she knew that her Freckles would be okay.

Chapter 18

For their first official date, Alex had taken Avery to the rooftop of a modern art museum where they sat, had a picnic and watched the stars. It was both a great distraction for the freckled girl and a romantic night. Alex had decorated the place with roses and candles and had even baked chocolate chip cookies for the curly-haired girl that was the apple of her eye.

About a week later, the word had spread about Alex and Avery's courtship and those who hadn't heard about it from the encounter between Avery and Carson definitely knew now. In that week, Avery's status had gone from not only being the girl that broke Carson Armani's heart but to also being the girl that managed to tie down Alex Rivers. And even though she didn't like it, those two titles made her somewhat popular throughout the school.

Life had been rough without Carson, no doubt, and Alex had done her best to keep her mind off of the best friend shaped hole in Avery's chest. But sometimes, the best course of action in life is just to wait.

"Hi," Alex wrapped her arms around the freckled girl from behind, planting a kiss to the crook of her neck. Avery blushed at the public display of affection from her...romantic companion. She couldn't refer to her as her 'girlfriend' because she didn't think that's what they were yet. Were they? Alex hadn't asked her.

Was it too 50's for her to wait for the tall girl to ask her to be her girlfriend? No. If it were the 50's, chances are they probably wouldn't even be dating due to all the homophobia.

"Hi," Avery said shyly. She went up on her tiptoes and gave the brunette a quick peck on the cheek before glancing around to make sure no one saw.

"You are adorable," the brunette said slowly with a broad smile. She was leaned up against Carson's locker as she gazed down adoringly at the freckled girl. The smile was reciprocated before it faded away when Avery spotted her ex-best friend walking towards them, surrounded by some of his football friends and with Marigold by his side. The sight brought a pang to her chest and she looked down on the floor before turning to her locker and continuing to replace her books.

"Excuse me," the brunet boy said icily after he cleared his throat. Alex removed herself from his locker begrudgingly, sending a glare his way. She had wanted to send a sucker punch to his nose and her hands balled into tight fists before relaxing themselves. She had to remind herself that hurting Carson would only hurt Avery, and she would never want to harm the curly-haired girl.

The short girl had finished doing what she needed to do but tried to keep herself busy so her eyes wouldn't wander off to Carson as she felt her tears spring to them. When he was finished, Carson closed his locker with a little more force than necessary and walked off, Marigold staying behind.

"Avery," she called to the freckled girl, attracting her attention. Instinctively, Alex went to her side and snaked a hand around her waist.

"You gave me such a tough time because you thought that I might hurt Carson. I just want you to think about the irony," she said with a smug look. She twirled her ginger ponytail with a sickeningly sweet smile before she made a move to walk away.

After she let her words sink in, her plan to make a spectacular exit was thwarted when Alex grabbed her by the arm and shoved her into one of the nearby lockers. The redhead winced at the pain in her back and the brunette bunched up the fabric of her shirt as she pinned her down.

"I may not be able to touch Armani because of Avery, but you're a fucking fool if you think you're off-limits too," Alex growled between gritted teeth. The football star was no match for the tall girl as she tried to get away from her. For added emphasis, Alex punched the area of a locker that was next to her head causing her to whimper.

In an attempt to calm down her lover, one of Avery's hands reached up to the brunette's shoulder and gave it a gentle squeeze. With one last shove, Alex removed her hands from where they held Marigold, allowing the girl to scurry off in the direction her boyfriend disappeared to like a scared dog with its tail between its legs. The tall girl then turned to the freckled one, catching her cheeks between her palms as she tried to read the look in her eyes.

"I'm fine," Avery reassured when she caught on to what Alex was doing. "Though I don't know whether to feel disappointed in you or to find that hot."

"I'd prefer the latter," Alex said with a smirk, slinging her arm over Avery's shoulder as she began to walk her to her class, "I was only protecting your honour, Freckles."

"Thank you, my Princess Charming."

****

"So you guys really stopped talking to Sam, huh?" Avery clarified as she sat down at the indoor lunch table with Alex, Jason and Kaden. The weather was now too cold for them to have lunch outdoors. She had only started sitting with the group a couple of days ago when Alex noticed that she was sitting by herself after the blowout with Carson. The brunette had pleaded with her to sit with her friends despite Avery's statements that she wasn't lonely. Now all four of them got along splendidly, especially since she hadn't seen Sam since the incident.

"What he did was dickish and his excuse sucked balls," Kaden said, words muffled by the mozzarella sticks he had stuffed in his mouth. He let out a gasp, nearly choking on his food in the process, "O.M.G was that a pun? Everything that I just said was related to penises."

Jason shook his head when the smaller boy looked over at him in excitement.

"What was his excuse?"

"Some shit about how he's protective of the group and he didn't want you intruding," Alex said nonchalantly. She slipped her hand around Avery's waist and brought her in closer to her without batting an eye or even looking in her direction. The freckled girl wasn't even sure if she noticed what she did and that made her blush.

"Yeah, but we all think it's because he used to have a crush on Alex back in middle school," Kaden spoke up again before he added, "You guys are cute."

Avery looked up at the tall girl, a sliver of jealousy slipping by. "Did you know about that?"

Alex only shrugged before she looked down at the shorter girl and sent her a reassuring smile, "Yeah I did. We never spoke about it because he knew it wasn't gonna go anywhere."

"But middle school was ages ago," Avery looked back to Kaden. "Why would affect how he acts now?"

"Feelings stick," he shrugged.

Jason rolled his eyes, quickly getting annoyed with the topic at hand. He had never been one to enjoy conversations about drama.

"Eat up, love," Alex said softly and nudged Avery's shoulder when she realised the younger girl had barely touched her pasta. She had lost her appetite. For some reason, she felt bad about the fact that Sam's ex-best friend's had stopped talking to him. If she hadn't had a panic attack, things would be fine between them by now. He'd only get a slap on the wrist like 'Hey Sam, that's not cool. Stop talking to her like that, you're being a dick'. But because her reaction was much more serious, his consequence was much more serious.

"I have two chocolate chip cookies for you in my bag, if you eat more," the brunette taunted her, causing Avery to pick up her fork once more. "That's my girl."

Alex's words brought a heavy blush to the freckled girl's cheeks. Jason's eyes widened and Kaden nearly choked, again.

"So it's official then. She's your girl girl?" Long questioned Alex.

"If she'll have me."

Avery's previous dark cloud of guilt suddenly disappeared as she felt her heart bloom with joy. It wasn't extravagant, the way she asked her. Hell, it wasn't even a question. It was casual but heartfelt at the same time and Avery loved it. There was no doubt in her mind that Alex brought her nothing but happiness.

"Of course!" she exclaimed giddily, attracting the attention of those who were nearby. For once, not giving a shit about who was watching or judging, she wrapped her arms around the back of Alex's neck and brought her down for a passionate kiss. And for the both of them, it felt like everything was going to be alright.

Chapter 19

"**M**aman, Papa. J'suis lesbi-enne."

The noise made by cutlery on plates ceased, causing Avery to cringe. The Christmas music in the background seemed almost haunting as it played quietly but was easily heard through the pin-drop silence. What did she expect, coming out during Christmas dinner?

Alex cleared her throat and wiped her mouth with a napkin, trying to cut through the awkwardness in the room.

"Pardon?" Mr Toussaint spoke up. Mrs Toussaint kept quiet and stared at her plate. This wasn't news for her, but her daughter's timing was definitely unexpected.

"Et," Avery stumbled but continued, "Alex n'est pas seulement mon amie. She's my girlfriend." {And Alex is not just my friend}

The brunette didn't know if she should say something or do something at this moment in time, but she knew she had to support her girlfriend. She placed her napkin on the table after some hesitation and stood alongside the freckled girl, holding her hand and giving it a reassuring squeeze.

"C'est genial, Doux-Doux. Can we all just sit down and eat now?" Mrs Toussaint chimed in. {That's great, sweetie}

"That's it?" Avery asked warily. She turned her head to look at her father who still seemed speechless, his eyes trained on the girls' entwined hands.

He seemed to get over his apparent shock as he shook his head before he spoke. "You are happy?" he asked, his thick accent coming through.

Avery looked up at the tall, brunette that stood next to her and felt her heart light up like their Christmas tree. She nodded fervently, not moving her gaze, "Very."

"Then I am happy."

The freckled girl turned her head and smiled warmly at her father, who just as quickly returned the expression. With that, she went back to her seat and dug into her half-finished meal, she and Alex still holding hands underneath the table.

The brunette leaned over to her and whispered, "You did it, baby. I'm so proud of you."

"Thank you for being here," Avery whispered back, before giving her girlfriend a peck on the lips. Milo yipped when he looked up from his food bowl, tilting his head in confusion at the girls' connected mouths.

The brunette rolled her eyes after they parted, "Why does he always do that every time we kiss? Have you realized that? Because I know I'm not crazy. Your dog has a lesbian fetish."

"He's my therapy dog, he has to watch me to make sure I'm okay. He probably senses my heart rate increase or something like that."

"Dogs do not have supersonic hearing."

"Maybe not, but they have really good hearing."

"Well, he should be used to me kissing you by now," Alex playfully folded her arms.

"Just let him watch, what's the worst that could happen?" Avery defended Milo.

"It's creepy!"

The Toussaints watched the young couple bicker with smiles on their faces, occasionally sharing a glance. They were probably thinking about the same thing. The spark in their daughter's eyes that was never there before they had met Alex.

"Now, now girls. If you want dessert, you'll have to finish your dinner first," Mrs Toussaint spoke to the 18-year-old young women as if they were children. Avery dug in without hesitation after hearing her mother's words.

Alex let out a laugh when the freckled girl finally came up for breath. There was gravy smeared across her mouth from how quickly she attempted to eat her roast beef. The girl's eyebrows came together in confusion and her bottom lip jutted out. "What?" she asked.

The brunette only shook her head and handed her a napkin.

"Nothing. You look so cute when you're confused."

Chapter 20

"Three!"

"Two!"

"One!"

"Happy New Year!"

The crowd burst into cheers as confetti rained from the ceiling. Alex grabbed Avery by the waist, swung her around and leaned her downwards, holding her firmly in place as she kissed her. The freckled girl giggled in their kiss and snaked her arms around Alex's neck, playing in her long hair.

When the brunette brought her up for breath, Avery sighed contently before she smirked. "Have I ever told you that you look so sexy with your hair down?" Sure it wasn't completely down all the way, Alex left that for when they were alone together, but it was in a half-up-half-down style that looked absolutely gorgeous on her and Avery was more than happy with that.

"You may have mentioned it once or twice," the tall girl responded cheekily before tugging the freckled girl's hand towards the dance floor.

Avery felt a strong sense of déjà vu as she walked through Alex's house weaving around hundreds of sweaty bodies that were dancing against each other. This time, though, it was under different circumstances. For instance, instead of isolating herself on the deck she was inside the party, dancing with her girlfriend.

"Could I get you something to drink first?" Alex asked, voice now raised to be heard above the loud music.

"Sure. But remember, no alcohol!" Avery responded, voice equally as loud.

"Okay, I'll be back. Stay right here!"

The freckled girl nodded before she started to sway in timing with the music, eventually starting to bop and dance around as she enjoyed the beat. One would think Alex had to drag her by the ankles to this New Year's party, but surprisingly it didn't take much convincing. Avery felt as if she was in a good place, her confidence was growing and her anxiety was under control. What would be the harm in following her girlfriend to a party at her own house; a house that she'd been to plenty of times? If it ever became too much, she knew where to find Alex's room and how to get inside Alex's secret room. Most importantly, she knew that the brunette would be right there with her, allowing her to stare into her stunning green eyes.

A few taps on her shoulder caught her attention and she swivelled around to face the offender. Surprisingly, or not so surprisingly, it was Carson.

"Hey!" he spoke up so she could hear.

"Hey!" Avery stopped dancing and looked up at him.

"How are you?!"

"I'm good, actually!" she smiled sheepishly, eyes darting to the ground. She was surprised at the lack of guilt that she felt when she said those words. But, they were the truth; she'd been growing and she felt better than she had before.

"Can I talk to you...outside?!"

"I can't. I have to stay here," she could now stop shouting above the music because the song had changed and so had the tempo.

"It'll be for just a quick sec."

"I'm sorry, Carson. You had so many opportunities to talk to me before. You even know where I live," Avery said before turning her back to him in an attempt to end the conversation.

"Please!" He was persistent, she knew that. Carson wasn't one to just give up. If he had been, he wouldn't have made it so far to be the football star that he was. She bit her lip and balled her hands into fists.

"Just a quick chat," he pleaded.

Maybe it was the pull of the five years of friendship, the desperation in his voice or the compelling urge to tie a neat bow on the package of her story, but she turned back around to face him.

"A quick chat," she reiterated with her eyes narrowed. Carson's eyes lit up before he started walking, gesturing for Avery to follow him and she did. They twisted and turned so as to prevent a collision with the multiple bodies that were in their path.

Soon enough, they were on the porch. The same porch that the freckled girl found herself on about three months ago, at a party like this one. But instead of Alex joining her out here, she was joining Carson.

The blond boy took a deep breath in before he spoke, suddenly feeling nervous with the weight of Avery's expectant eyes on him. "I'm sorry."

"Oh," the curly-haired girl replied, albeit sarcastically.

"I was so harsh to you when I didn't need to be. You only made one mistake in five years of friendship and I made you feel like hell for it," he looked to the floor.

"My relationship is my business," Avery bit out, taking the chance to tell him what she wished she had before. She had had time to think about it and the longer that she did, the less guilty she felt. "I don't have to tell you who I have a crush on and who I'm hanging out with, that's not what our friendship is about. Most best friends don't even tell each other everything the way we do."

"Well, you didn't have to lie about it," Carson bit back, suddenly feeling very defensive.

"It was just one thing, Carson! I was only lying to you about how I started talking to Alex. Everything else was lying by omission. Either way, people lie all the fucking time, Carson. Grow up!" she snapped as frustration ran through her blood. Avery sighed and continued in a much calmer voice, "I'm not saying what I did was okay, but I'm saying it didn't deserve what you put me through."

The tall boy took a step back in surprise, shaking his head, "You don't curse."

"I do curse, just not in English."

"She's changing you, Aves, don't you see?"

It was Avery's turn to take a step back but in hurt. "Yeah, for the better."

Carson used his hand to gesture between them, his eyes narrowed, "How is this better?"

"I'm not 'Avery: The Wallflower' anymore. I'm 'Avery: The Reader, the girl who likes chocolate chip cookies and autumn'. I'm 'Avery: the girl who can stand up for herself, who can go to a party and have a good time'. I'm 'Avery: the girl who has anxiety but doesn't let it hold her back'. I'm learning so many things about myself and doing things I didn't know I could all because of her. I'm not living in my own bubble anymore, I'm not holding myself back. I don't let the negative things about me define me anymore. For once I don't feel like something is weighing me down. And that's a change for the better if I do say so myself."

"Well, you're not like the Avery I know," the boy said with a huff, guilt and sadness written in his eyes. If he had looked a little harder, he would've have seen that the Avery he knew was still there, only evolved.

"And that's okay," the freckled girl replied softly, "Sometimes to grow, we have to leave other people behind."

With that, she walked away. She didn't know if she had done the right thing, said the right thing or if she should have just accepted his apology instead of causing drama. But there was one thing she did know- she felt proud of herself. And it was a damn good feeling.

Maybe- hopefully- she and Carson would be friends again, but she had a feeling that at this stage in her life it wasn't right for them to be. They both had very differ-ent ideas about what she should be when the decision should be hers, right?

Alex: Hey, where are you? Avery read when she checked her phone on her way through the crowd. She quickly typed and sent a response.

A: Heading towards the room

A: Meet me there

****

"And so I did it. I just walked away," Avery finished telling the brunette about her encounter with Carson.

Alex played the remaining chords of the piece gracefully, her eyes trained on her girlfriend who sat gorgeously on top of the black piano.

"That was beautiful, by the way," the freckled girl added, referring to Alex's music.

"Are you sure you even heard it during your wild storytelling?" the tall girl smirked.

"Are you sure you even heard my story during your wild playing?" she retorted.

"Yes I did, but you don't need me to tell you how proud I am of you. I always am. I knew you had it in you, it was just for you to find it."

"Now," Alex patted the seat next to her on the piano bench, "Come here Freckles. What do you want me to play next for you?"

Avery hopped off the piano and walked over to stand behind her girlfriend, her fingers took hold of the scrunchie that held the top half of her hair and removed it, setting it all free. She ran her hands through the long dark hair and massaged her scalp, pleased to hear the tall girl let out a blissful sigh in response.

"Seeing Stars by Børns, the piano version. And I want you to sing it too," the freckled girl requested after some contemplation.

"Quite bossy today, are we? You stick up for yourself once and now you run the world," Alex teased.

"Just play," Avery said with a slight smile, swatting Alex's arm playfully as she went to sit down next to her.

The brunette complied with her lover's wishes, beginning to play the beautiful introduction to the song.

[There should be a GIF or video here. Update the app now to see it.]

Saw her walking on the side of the road on the sidewalk chalk from my balcony window

First sight she made me look twice 'cause I'd never seen someone walk as light as the wind blows

I called out to try and get your name, quickly wrote a love letter turned it into an airplane

You looked up and that was enough 'cause you let out all the butterflies that couldn't be contained.

Avery snuggled into the brunette's side and closed her eyes as the familiar, melodious voice kissed her eardrums.

You've got me seeing stars brighter than ever, shining just like diamonds do.

I know that in time it could be all ours, brighter than ever

Your love is such a dream come true;

I know, I know, I know I need you.

There's a love I've been keeping inside and you're the missing puzzle piece that I've been trying to find

Hey girl, you've got me learning to fly

You've got me higher than a kite and I've been painting the sky

Some dreams never do come true

Some love doesn't hit the target

But my dreams are reality now and you're the one I've been dreaming about.

Avery couldn't help but think about how those lyrics ran true for the way she felt about Alex and her face warmed to hear the brunette sing them. She wrapped her arms around the tall girl's neck and peppered kisses to her cheek and jaw as she began to hum to the tune of the song.

"You're amazing," the freckled girl muttered between her kisses.

In the ending notes of the song, Alex hit a key she apparently hadn't used in a while as it caused unearthed dust to spring upon the two.

"Oh my god," Avery gasped, a small smile tugging at the corner of her lips.

"I haven't dusted this thing in a while," the brunette admitted sheepishly but donning a small smile of her own. When Avery didn't respond for a while, Alex looked over to her in concern. The curly-haired girl's face was contorted in a weird expression before she sneezed.

On Alex.

The two stared at each other long and hard, Avery's face red in embarrassment but trying to stifle a laugh. Her attempts were to no avail as she let out a strangled chuckle.

And the girls erupted into a fit of giggles.

Lightning Source UK Ltd.
Milton Keynes UK
UKHW020709270223
417728UK00015B/1092